HELP!
I'M TRAPPED IN SUMMER CAMP

TODD STRASSER

SCHOLASTIC INC.

New York Toronto London Auckland Sydney
Mexico City New Delhi Hong Kong Buenos Aires

Help! I'm Trapped in the First Day of Summer Camp,
ISBN-13: 978-0-590-02965-0, ISBN-10: 0-590-02965-7. Copyright © 1997 by Todd Strasser.

Help! I'm Trapped in My Camp Counselor's Body,
ISBN-13: 978-0-590-03272-8, ISBN-10: 0-590-03272-0. Copyright © 1998 by Todd Strasser.

12 11 10 9 8 7 6 5 4 3 2 1   7 8 9 10 11/0

Printed in the U.S.A.   40

This edition created exclusively for Barnes & Noble, Inc.

2007 Barnes & Noble Books

ISBN-13: 978-0-7607-9688-7
ISBN-10: 0-7607-9688-2

This edition first printing, August 2007

Contents

HELP!
I'M TRAPPED IN THE
FIRST DAY OF SUMMER CAMP

To Geoff, bon voyage!

1

"Just be yourself," said my sister, Jessica. "Just try your best," said my father.

"Just remember to brush your teeth," said my mother.

We were sitting in the kitchen, having breakfast. They were giving me advice before I went away to camp for the first time.

"Thanks, guys, I'll remember all that." I yawned and stretched my arms.

Mom narrowed her eyes and studied me closely. "You look tired. Didn't you sleep last night?"

"Sure, I did," I said, even though I'd hardly slept at all.

"No way," said Jessica. "He was up all night tossing and turning in bed. Can you believe the great Jake Sherman is scared about going away to camp for the first time?"

"Am not," I said.

1

"Are too," she shot back. "I know you, Jake. You're totally freaked."

"I don't see why he should be scared," Mom said. "After all, he's only going for a month and his two best friends will be there with him."

"But Camp Walton has a rule against friends sharing bunks," Jessica said. "Jake's little play pals Josh and Andy will be in other cabins."

"But they'll be at the same camp," Dad said. "They'll get to see each other."

"Doesn't matter," my sister said. "What matters is who Jake shares his cabin with. What happens when they find out what a dork he is? What if they all hate him?"

"Hon?" said my mother to my sister.

"You guys never went to camp when you were kids," Jessica went on. "You don't have a clue how scary going for the first time can be. I mean, knowing Jake, he'll probably do something really dumb on the first day. What if he comes off looking like a fool? Once he's got that label, he's finished. Believe me, I'd be freaked too if I were Jake. This could turn out to be the worst summer of his life."

"*Ahem!*" Mom cleared her throat loudly. "Are you *sure* Jake needs to hear this?"

"Absolutely," Jessica insisted. "Don't you remember what happened to me on my first day at camp? I tripped during a ball game and got a face full of mud. For the rest of the summer they called me Mud Face. It was a total bummer. I hated it. If you ask me, I don't even know why they call it summer *camp*. Summer *prison* is more like it. It can be pure tor — "

"*Hon!*" Mom blurted. "Please stop now. You're scaring Jake."

Jessica blinked and looked surprised.

"Yeah," I said. "What do you want me to do? Stay home with you?"

Jessica's eyes widened. "No!"

Mom smiled. "I think Jessica just got a little carried away. I'm sure this is going to be a great month for Jake."

"It's definitely going to be a great month for *me* without my skinkbrain brother around," said Jessica.

"You may be surprised," said Mom. "You may actually discover you miss Jake."

"Right." Jessica smirked. "I may also discover that I have an extra eye growing out the back of my head and that I love eating chocolate-covered cockroaches, but somehow I doubt it."

My sister was going to spend the summer at the town pool being a junior lifeguard, whatever that meant.

"Listen, guys," I said. "I'm sure everything's going to be cool at Camp Walton, and I'm gonna have a great time."

"That's the spirit." Mom gave me an encouraging smile.

"Just remember, Jake," said my father, "even if you're completely miserable and unhappy, you have to stay. After the first week, they don't give refunds if you leave early. So no matter how bad it gets, you're stuck there."

Mom sighed at Dad. "I know you mean well, dear, but I'm not sure that's the most positive approach to take."

"Look, Mom, Dad," I said. "It really doesn't matter. I — "

Ding dong! The doorbell rang.

Groof! Groof! Lance, our yellow Labrador retriever, started barking.

Jessica got up, went to the kitchen window, and looked outside. "Oh, my gosh! You're not going to believe this!"

2

Iwent to the kitchen window. Outside my friends Alex Silver, Julia Saks, and Amber Sweeny were standing on the sidewalk in front of our house. They were holding up a large banner made out of a bed sheet. The banner said:

HAVE A GREAT TIME AT CAMP
DON'T COME
~~HURRY BACK~~

"I guess I'm not the only one who's *not* going to miss you," Jessica quipped.

"You're a real riot, Jess," I grumbled, and went to the front door.

As soon as I stepped outside, my friends reached into their pockets and pulled out giant handkerchiefs they must have torn from another sheet. They pretended to cry and blow their noses.

"Gee, guys," I said. "I didn't know you cared."

5

"We don't," Alex said as he dabbed his eyes. "It must be an allergy or something."

Julia handed me a shoe box. "We took up a collection and got this for you."

"What is it?" I asked.

"A survival kit," said Amber.

I opened the box. Inside was a bag of party balloons, a can of Cheese Whiz, a pack of crackers, and a small box of Band Aids.

"I can understand the Cheese Whiz, crackers, and Band Aids," I said. "But what's with the balloons?"

"You can't survive camp without them," said Alex.

"What are you talking about?" I said.

"Balloons are an essential component in the manufacture of water balloons," he explained. "Camp without water balloons is like a Big Mac without fries."

"Thanks, I'll remember that." I slid the box under my arm. "You guys sure know how to make a kid feel good."

"So when do you leave?" Julia asked.

I checked my watch. "Any minute now."

Amber pointed at my T-shirt. "It's really called Camp Walton?"

"No," I said. "It's called Camp Big-Chewy-Booger but they ran out of those T-shirts so I have to wear this."

Julia and Amber grinned, but Alex had a

6

pained expression on his face. "Seriously, Jake, what do you want to go to camp for?"

"I guess because I've never tried it," I said.

"You've never tried bungee jumping off the Golden Gate Bridge either," said Amber. "You gonna try that next?"

"Probably not," I said.

"So what are we supposed to do for the next month while you're gone?" Alex asked.

"Uh . . . sit around and miss me?" I suggested.

"Fat chance." Julia smirked.

"Just remember, dude," Alex said. "New experiences can be dangerous. Look what happened to Icarus."

Amber frowned. *"Who?"*

"Don't you remember that Greek dude who made wings out of wax?" Alex asked. "He flew too close to the sun and the wax melted and he fell back to earth and did the big splat."

"If I make any wax wings in arts and crafts, I'll remember not to fly too close to the sun," I said.

Just then Dad, Mom, and Jessica came out.

"Time to go, Jake," said my father as he lugged my big green duffle bag to our van and dumped it in the back. The rear of the van dipped and the springs squeaked. Then Mom and Jessica got in.

My friends grew silent. It was time for me to leave. Suddenly I actually did start to feel a little nervous. Then I had an idea.

"Hey, you guys want to come with us to the

place where the camp bus picks me up?" I asked.

"Not exactly the most exciting offer we've ever had," Alex muttered.

"Where it is, anyway?" asked Amber.

"The parking lot of Super Donut," I said.

"Would your parents get us some donuts if we went?" Julia asked.

"Uhh . . . I don't see why not," I said.

My friends started to grin.

"Suddenly I want to be with Jake until the very last second," said Alex.

"Wait, Jake." My father rolled down his window and stuck his head out. "Don't forget we have to pick up Josh and Andy and all their stuff. That won't leave much room."

"Aw, darn, and I thought we were going to get something good out of this," Julia said with a sigh.

"Sorry, guys." I waved at my friends and got into the van. "Guess I'll see you when I get back."

3

We picked up Josh and Andy at their houses and threw their duffle bags in the van. My friends and I sat together in the back. They weren't exactly happy campers.

"I can't believe I'm going to this dumb camp," Josh groaned.

"Yeah," Andy agreed. "I mean, what's wrong with hanging around here and complaining that there's nothing to do? That's what we do *every* summer."

"Look, guys, this could be really good for us," I said.

"Really good for *you*, maybe," Josh grumbled. "Not for me. I'm the chubby kid. You ever notice in every camp movie there's a chubby kid with six candy bars in his pocket who can't make it around the bases without stopping to catch his breath. Well, that's me."

"No way," I said. "You're a good athlete."

"You and Andy know that," said Josh. "But no

one else does. Everyone's gonna look at me and think of the chubby kid in those movies. They're never gonna give me a chance. I never should've told my parents you were going to camp. Then they wouldn't be making me go."

"Yeah." Andy nodded. "This really bites."

"What's *your* problem?" I asked him. "You're not chubby."

"I've got braces," Andy said.

"So?"

"So they're gonna give me a dumb nickname," Andy said. "Everybody gets a nickname in camp. Mine's gonna be something really stupid like railroad lips or terminator teeth."

"You guys worry too much," I said. "Camp Walton's going to be totally cool."

But Andy and Josh didn't look convinced.

"You guys know what a super-wedgy is?" Andy asked.

Josh and I shook our heads. "Never heard of it."

"My cousin told me about it," Andy explained. "They only have them at camps. The camp cabins have rafters. So they take a rope and put one end through your belt. The other end goes over the rafter. Then they haul you up."

"Eww!" Josh winced in imagined pain and reached for the van's door handle. "Forget it, I'm not going."

"Hold it, you guys," I said. "I think you're just

10

nervous because they won't let us bunk together. But maybe that's good. We're always together, so this'll be different."

"Sure," Josh moaned. "We'll all get super-wedgied in a different cabin."

"I'll tell you what will be different," Andy said in a low voice so my parents and sister wouldn't hear. "Being away from Mr. Dorkson's dumb machine. At least we won't have to worry about switching bodies with anything for a while."

Josh pretended to look surprised. "Gee, Andy, I thought you liked being Jake's dog."

"Very funny," Andy replied sourly.

Just a few months before, Andy and my dog Lance had accidentally switched bodies. Lance, in Andy's body, went to regular school while Andy, in Lance's body, went to obedience school.

"So listen, guys," I said. "Did you get flashlights?"

"Oh, yeah." Josh opened his day pack and took out a long black flashlight. "It's made of aluminum. Not only does it work as a flashlight, but if I run into any bears in the woods, I can whack 'em on the head."

"Cool," I said, getting out my dual action light. "Mine not only has a spotlight. It has a wide-area fluorescent that blinks automatically so that if I get lost in the woods at night a search plane can find me."

We both turned to Andy, to see what kind of

flashlight he'd gotten. Andy opened his day pack and took out a huge thing with a pistol grip and curly black cord leading to a separate battery pack.

"Oh, wow!" I gasped. "That's incredible."

Andy grinned sheepishly. "It's called the SuperBeam. One million candle power. Twenty-five times brighter than the high beams on this van. This thing could light up a whole baseball stadium."

Only Josh didn't look impressed. "It may be bright, but what good is that going to do if you run into a bear?"

"I'll just have to blind him," Andy replied with a smile.

4

The camp bus hadn't arrived yet when we got to the Super Donut. Mom, Dad, and Jessica went inside to buy donuts. Josh, Andy, and I hung out in the parking lot. Josh mumbled something under his breath.

"What?" I didn't quite catch what he'd said.

Josh and Andy winked at each other and grinned.

"What'd you say?" I asked. "I didn't get it."

"I said, 'The fungus says, "What?"'" Josh spoke more clearly.

"What?" I said.

Josh and Andy grinned some more.

Then I got it and felt my face turn red. "Very funny, guys."

"But you have to admit it's a good one," Andy said.

"Yeah, right." I started to look around, scoping out the other campers.

"Check out those guys." Andy pointed at three

kids throwing a baseball around on the other side of the parking lot. They could all throw really hard and far.

"Serious jock types," Josh said.

"The cool guys," Andy added warily. "Watch out."

"Maybe they're okay," I said.

"Sure, and maybe I'm the frog prince," Andy said. "They're too cool. That's why they're over there throwing the ball around. They want to make sure everyone sees them. You see any parents with them?"

Josh and I shook our heads.

"Of course not," Andy said. "They're letting everyone know that they're too cool to have parents. Not like the rest of us dweebazoids waiting around for the bus with Mom and Dad."

As Andy said that, he pointed at the kids who *were* waiting with their parents. In a weird way it seemed like he was right. The kids who hung with their parents did seem dorkier. Their clothes and hair didn't look as cool.

I looked back at the cool guys. They were definitely wearing the coolest clothes and sneakers, and they had the coolest hair. Then I compared my friends to them. Unfortunately it was hard for Josh to look cool because he was chubby and his face was always red. And Andy rarely looked cool because he had braces and a few zits.

Then I looked down at my own sneakers and clothes. I thought I looked pretty cool too. Could I fit in with those cool guys?

Mom, Dad, and Jessica came out of the Super Donut with three yellow and red travel boxes of donuts.

"There is one *good* thing about parents bringing you to the bus," I said. "They supply the donuts."

"You're right about that," Josh admitted and patted his day pack. "Sure beats Cheese Whiz on crackers."

Andy looked surprised. "You brought that too?"

"So did I," I said.

"It's the universal emergency camp food," said Josh.

My parents and sister arrived with the donuts.

"How come so many boxes, Mrs. Sherman?" Andy asked, eyeing the donuts hungrily.

"We're going to take one box home with us," Mom replied. "The second box we'll eat here, and the third is for Jake to take on the bus and share with all his new friends."

Andy grinned and put his lips close to my ear. *"You're going to share your donuts on the bus,"* he teased. *"Aw, isn't that cute?"*

"Drop dead." I gave him a poke with my elbow.

Meanwhile, Dad opened the first box of donuts. "Come and get 'em, boys."

Josh, Andy, and I each took a donut, then walked a dozen feet away and stood by ourselves.

"Is it my breath?" Dad asked with a concerned look.

As usual, brain-girl Jessica figured out the real reason. "No, Dad, it's Jake. He's afraid that if he stands with his parents he won't look cool to the other kids."

"Then maybe we should go," said Mom.

That made me feel bad.

"Naw, it's okay," I said. "You guys can stay."

"We can stay," said Jessica. "But we're not allowed to get too close to you, right?"

"Right." I nodded.

Jessica rolled her eyes. "Pathetic."

"Oh, look." Mom pointed at a family on the other side of the parking lot. "Isn't that the Peelings?"

We looked across the parking lot at a tall kid with glasses and black hair. He was wearing a white Camp Walton T-shirt and green-and-red-plaid shorts. Some lady, probably his mother, was making him stand still while she reached up and combed his hair.

"You're right," Dad said. "We haven't seen them in years."

"Now that I think of it, they had a boy the same age as Jake," said Mom. "Let's go say hello."

16

Mom and Dad walked across the parking lot. Meanwhile, the kid's mother was still combing his hair.

"Can you believe she's doing that *in public?*" Andy whispered.

"What's worse is that he's *letting* her do it," Josh added. "That kid must be a triple mega-dorkazoid."

We watched as my parents introduced themselves to the dorkazoid's parents. A few moments later, my mother turned and waved across the parking lot to me. "Jake, hon? Come on over. There's someone here we'd like you to meet."

"Tough break, Jake." Andy grimly clapped his hand on my shoulder. "You just became a dorkazoid by association."

5

As I walked slowly across the parking lot toward my parents and the Peelings, I glanced back at the cool kids playing ball, and hoped they weren't watching. Mr. Peeling was a tall, gawky-looking guy like his son. He had one of the longest necks and the biggest Adam's apple I'd ever seen, and sort of reminded me of a giraffe. Mrs. Peeling was a large woman with a big blond hairdo and lots of jewelry around her neck and wrists. Definitely more of a hippo.

I could just imagine what the son of a giraffe and hippo would be like. Definitely not cool.

"Jake," Mom said, "I want you to meet Mr. and Mrs. Peeling and their son, Peter. They used to be our neighbors in the city. We just found out that you and Peter are both in cabin B-13. Isn't that wonderful?"

Peter held out his hand. It was pretty limp, and he had awful long fingernails for a boy. He didn't look at me when we shook hands.

"Oh, I think this is sooo wonderful!" Mrs. Peeling gushed. "Petey's been sooo worried that he wouldn't know anyone at camp. We had to force him to go. If it was up to him, he'd just sit in front of the TV all day and — "

"Uh, Mom," Peter interrupted. He had a pained look on his face. "I really don't think you have to tell them all that."

"Why not Petey?" his mom asked. "It's true, isn't it?"

Peter's face turned red and I felt bad for him. His mother sure wasn't helping things by embarrassing him like that.

"This is your lucky day, Petey," Mr. Peeling said. "Jake looks like a nice boy. I'm sure you two are going to be best friends by the time camp is over."

An awkward moment passed while neither Peter nor I knew what to say. Just then I happened to look down at his feet. Peter was wearing sandals. He had the longest toenails I'd ever seen.

They were almost lethal weapons!

I straightened up. Peter might have been the greatest guy on earth, but there was no way I was going to be friends with anyone who wore sandals and had killer toenails.

We all heard the squeak of brakes. A green bus pulled into the parking lot. It looked like an old school bus that had been repainted.

"We better go get your stuff, Jake," Dad said. He and Mom said good-bye to the Peelings.

Peter and I just nodded at each other.

"So what do you think of Peter?" Mom asked in a low voice as we walked back across the parking lot to the car.

"I don't know, Mom. He seems a little geeky."

"You'd be geeky too if you had Margaret Peeling for a mother," my father whispered.

"John!" Mom gasped under her breath. "That's not very nice."

"Well, maybe not, but it's the truth, isn't it?" Dad replied with a shrug.

Mom didn't answer. She turned to me. "Well, anyway, Jake. Since he's in the same cabin as you, it would be very nice if you two became friends."

"Sure, Mom," I said. But inside I was thinking, *No way!*

6

We got back to the van. All around us, parents were giving their kids last minute instructions. Or hugging them. Or, in Peter Peeling's case, combing his hair again. The three cool baseball players carried their duffle bags toward the bus. Their parents were nowhere in sight.

Mom spread her arms. "Can I give you a hug and a kiss good-bye, Jake?"

"Uh . . ." I took a step back and looked around, hoping that the cool guys weren't watching.

"Get with the program, Mom." Jessica smirked. "Cool kids don't even *have* mothers. As far as Jake's concerned, you've ceased to *exist.*"

Mom gave me a crooked smile and dropped her arms.

Dad held out his hand. "Then how about a manly shake?"

"Sure." I shook his hand.

"Put 'er there, Jake." Jessica held out her hand. I shook it.

Mom sighed and held out her hand as well. "I'm glad we can conclude this meeting in a businesslike manner," she said sarcastically as we shook. "Just don't forget to brush your teeth."

"Sure, Mom."

Josh and Andy had already gotten on the bus. I got my day pack and duffle bag out of the van. The day pack contained my flashlight, Discman, some CDs, and a bag of chips for the bus ride. The duffle bag weighed a ton.

As I trudged toward the bus, almost bent double by the weight of the duffle, Josh opened a window and stuck his head out. "What's in that thing?"

"Don't know. My mom packed it." With a grunt I heaved the duffle bag onto the luggage carrier welded to the back of the bus.

"Better hurry," Josh said. "Looks like you're the last one to get on."

He was right. All the other campers were already on the bus. I spun around to my parents and sister and gave them one last wave. "See you in a month."

"No rush," Jessica called back. She waved with her right hand. Her left hand was behind her back.

I climbed onto the bus. The doors closed behind me and the bus lurched into motion. As I looked out the window, Jessica brought her left hand from behind her back. She held up a red and yellow box of donuts.

My donuts!

Jessica rubbed her stomach and licked her lips. She'd stolen my donuts!

That slimeball!

7

The bus started to move. I was still standing in the front. I looked at the rows of faces in the seats. A lot of the kids were younger, a few were my age and a few were older. Some of them looked back at me. Others gazed out the windows. Still others were already talking to the kid they were sitting next to.

"You better get a seat, son," said an older guy, who was sitting right behind the bus driver. He was wearing glasses, a gray Camp Walton T-shirt, and holding a clipboard.

"Yo, Jake!" About halfway back, Andy waved at me. He was sitting next to Josh. I walked down the aisle toward them. As I got nearer I saw that the closest empty seat was in the row behind them, right next to . . . Peter Peeling.

Dork by association . . . Andy's words echoed in my ears. Part of me said "Don't sit there," but another part of me remembered what Mom had said

24

about being nice. Sitting with the guy on the bus couldn't hurt, could it?

I stopped next to Peter. He looked up at me and smiled a little.

I was just about to sit down in the seat next to him when a voice said, "Look out."

I followed the voice to the back of the bus. The three cool baseball players were sitting in the last row, watching me. They were all wearing headphones, listening to Discmans, and munching on Pringles.

"You really want to sit there?" one of them asked. He was short and stocky, with short black hair and a diamond stud in one ear.

I hesitated and looked down at Peter. He quickly looked away. His ears and cheeks were growing red.

"Hey, it's a free country," said another one of the cool guys in a mocking tone. He was the tallest of the three and had bushy blond hair.

"Yeah, but you gotta watch out for cooties," said the short guy.

The third guy said nothing. His hair was longer and light brown. He was wearing a leather thong around his neck with a single large bead in it.

Andy and Josh twisted around in their seat and looked at me with puzzled expressions.

"Aren't you going to sit?" Andy asked.

"Back there," I answered, and sat down in an

empty row halfway between Peter Peeling and the cool guys.

"Definitely a wise decision," said the short stocky guy with the earring.

"So what's your name?" asked the guy with the longer brown hair and the leather thong.

"Jake," I said. "What's yours?"

"Rick," the kid said.

"Dan," said the stocky kid with the dark hair.

"Zack," said the blond guy. "What cabin you in?"

"B-13," I said. "You?"

"The very same," said Rick, and the other two nodded to show they were in that cabin also.

"Should be a pretty cool group this year," said Dan.

"With one definite exception," added Zack, looking past me at Peter.

8

The bus went over a bump and I felt my eyes open. For a second I didn't know where I was. Then I realized I'd fallen asleep. I yawned and looked out the window. We were pulling into a big gravel parking lot. Other buses were already there and kids wearing white Camp Walton T-shirts were climbing out of them.

In the parking lot, older guys wearing gray Camp Walton T-shirts and carrying clipboards were talking to small groups of campers. In the background were some buildings made of brown logs, and behind them was a lake with a dock and some sailboats.

I rubbed my eyes and stretched.

"Have a nice nap, Sleeping Beauty?" someone asked.

I looked up into Zack's smiling face as he, Dan, and Rick filed down the aisle past me.

"Oh, yeah." I stretched and yawned again.

"See ya in the cabin," said Rick.

A moment later they passed Peter Peeling as he stood up. He picked up a white paper shopping bag that must have contained his bus stuff. The rest of us had day packs. The shopping bag was like Peter — hopelessly dorky.

"Cool bag," Zack said with a chuckle.

Peter didn't reply. He just bowed his head and wouldn't look Zack in the eye. He waited until they left the bus. When they were gone, he went down the aisle and got off.

That left three people on the bus: Josh, Andy, and me.

"How come you didn't sit with us?" Josh asked.

"Uh, well, I knew I was gonna sleep," I lied.

"Bull," Andy said. "You just didn't want to sit next to that Peeling kid. So, did you make friends with the cool guys?"

"Not really," I said, getting up.

"Well, there's still plenty of time," Andy said, as if he could read my mind.

Andy, Josh, and I went down the aisle. Outside the bus, the driver was pulling the duffle bags out of the luggage carrier. Peter Peeling got his bag and spoke to an older guy wearing a grey Camp Walton T-shirt. The guy checked his clipboard, then pointed toward a line of small wooden buildings, which must have been the cabins where we campers would live.

I saw the driver pull out my duffle bag and drop it to the ground with a thud. I went over and struggled to pick it up. Rick, Dan, and Zack were still waiting for theirs.

"What'd you put in there?" Dan, the stocky kid with the black hair, asked with a smile. "Bowling balls?"

I almost answered that I didn't know what was in the bag because my mom had packed for me. But I caught myself. Admitting your mom packed for you wasn't cool.

"I listen to a lot of heavy metal," I said.

Dan scowled, but Rick grinned. He was the one with the brown hair.

"*Heavy* metal?" he said. "That's funny. Are you a comedian?"

"Only when I'm awake," I said.

By now, Andy and Josh had gotten their duffle bags.

"So where's your cabin?" Andy asked me.

I pointed toward B-13.

"Bummer," he said. "Josh and I are that way." He pointed toward some cabins on the other side of a large field with some soccer goals and a baseball diamond.

"Guess I'll catch you guys later," I said, and started to lug my duffle bag toward my cabin.

Halfway to the cabin, Rick, Dan and Zack passed me. Their duffle bags looked a lot lighter.

"Come on, Sleeping Beauty, don't be such a slowpoke," Zack teased. He was the tall one with the bushy blond hair. I struggled to keep up with them. Ahead we could see Peter Peeling carrying his duffle and white shopping bag. All of a sudden the bottom of the shopping bag split and all the stuff inside spilled onto the grass. Peter dropped his duffle and started to pick up the items, which included a white plastic thing with a long, clear plastic tube attached to it.

Zack, Rick, and Dan paused to watch.

"Hey, guys, look," Zack said. "A Water Pik."

"Whoa." Dan grinned. "This guy takes serious care of his teeth."

"It's for my gums," Peter tried to explain.

"Gums, huh?" chuckled Dan. "Hey, maybe we should call him Gummi Bear."

"Yeah, that sounds right," agreed Zack. He turned to me. "What do *you* think, Sleeping Beauty?"

Suddenly the cool guys and Peter were looking at me, waiting for my reply. Peter winced at the nickname. I could just imagine him writing home and complaining that I'd agreed to call him Gummi Bear. His mother would probably call my mother and scream at her. But I wouldn't have to deal with that until I got home from camp. Right now I was just trying to survive the first fifteen minutes.

"Sounds okay to me." I shrugged and didn't look at Peter.

"So be it," Zack said. "See you in the cabin, *Gummi Bear.*"

The cool guys started toward the cabin. I glanced at Peter, but he wouldn't look at me.

"Hey, Sleeping Beauty!" Dan yelled back to me. "You coming or what?"

"Uh, yeah, I'm coming," I said, and followed.

9

Our cabin was pretty small. First you went up two wooden steps to a porch, and then inside through a creaking screen door. Three double decker bunk beds stood in the middle and back. A regular bed was placed near the screen door.

"That's for the counselor," Dan said. "We get the double deckers."

Thunk! I dropped my duffle bag next to the first double decker I came to.

"You don't want to take that one, Sleeping Beauty," Zack said. "Only the dweebs want to be close to the counselor."

"Come on back here with us," said Rick. "You can take the top of my bunk."

I dragged my duffle bag back to Rick's bunk bed and started to unpack. The bunks had thin mattresses, made up with white sheets and gray blankets.

The next camper to enter the cabin was Peter,

who put his stuff down on the bunk nearest the counselor's bed.

"It never fails," Zack said in a low voice. Dan smiled.

The last kid in the cabin was small and blond with a slight build. The only bed left was the top of Peter's double decker, and without a word the blond kid took it.

"It never fails?" Dan said it like a question this time and looked at Zack. I knew he was asking if Zack thought the blond kid was a dweeb, too. I was starting to get the feeling that Zack was the ringleader.

"Looks like it," Zack replied. He looked at me. "What do *you* think, Sleeping Beauty?"

Every time they spoke to me, I felt like I was being tested. Part of me thought it was stupid, but another part of me really wanted to pass the test.

"It's your call," I said with a shrug.

It took a while to get everything unpacked. The reason my duffle bag was so heavy was that my mother had packed enough underwear for me to change four times a day for a month and still have some left over.

While I shoved underwear in my cubby, the cool guys asked where I was from and I asked where they were from. But there was another question I really wanted to ask. Finally I got up the nerve.

"It seems like you guys are pretty good friends," I said. "I thought they had a rule against friends sharing cabins."

"It's not a real firm rule," Zack said. "If you get your parents to write a letter saying you might not come back if you can't be with your friends, the camp overlooks it really fast."

I wished I'd known that sooner. I would have given anything to be with Josh and Andy. Then I wouldn't have to worry about making new friends or being singled out as a dweeb.

A tall, lanky older guy with curly black hair came in. He was wearing a gray Camp Walton T-shirt, and said his name was Marty and that he was our counselor. He had an easygoing smile and looked pretty friendly. But when he focused on Zack, Dan, and Rick his expression changed.

"Don't I remember you three from last year?" Marty asked. "Didn't you three bunk together?"

"So?" Zack asked back.

It looked like Marty was going to say something, but he just shrugged and told the rest of us to introduce ourselves. That's how I found out the small blond kid's name was Lewis.

Marty showed us how the cabin worked. Outside was a clothesline where we could hang our wet bathing suits and damp towels to dry, and in back of the cabin was a hose for washing down our tennis shoes and anything else that got muddy.

Then Marty said he had to go down to the waterfront because he was also one of the swimming instructors. He said he'd come back later and take us over to the cafeteria for lunch. In the meantime we should finish unpacking and get to know each other. He added that there was a new tetherball game in the front of the cabin and we could play if we wanted.

After Marty left, Zack strolled to the front of the cabin and looked up at Lewis. The small blond kid was kneeling on his bunk, tacking pictures of racing cars to a rafter over his bed.

"Guess you're into cars, huh?" Zack asked.

Lewis nodded.

"*Small* cars, right?" Zack said.

"*Fast* cars," Lewis replied.

"*Small* fast cars, then," said Zack with a grin.

In the back of the cabin Dan snickered.

Lewis looked down at Zack, right into his eyes. "You think you're funny?"

Zack blinked. Lewis was challenging him, which was kind of interesting considering Zack was at least eight inches taller and probably weighed forty pounds more.

"Whoa, tough little guy," Dan said in a low voice.

"Mighty Mouse," said Zack with a smile. "Yeah, that's what we're gonna call you. So we got

Mighty Mouse and Gummi Bear in the first bunk."

Lewis turned back to his pictures and didn't say a word. Meanwhile, Peter had been sitting on the lower bunk, quietly unpacking his stuff.

Now Zack turned to him. "Hey, Gummi Bear, wanna play some tetherball?"

Every time one of the cool guys spoke to Peter, he seemed to shiver slightly. He always bowed his head, and never looked them in the eye.

"Uh, I'm not sure."

Zack put his hands on his hips. "What are you, some kind of wuss?"

In the back, Dan snickered again. I noticed that Rick was silent and didn't join his friends when they picked on kids.

"I . . . I don't know what tetherball is," Peter said.

"How can you not know what tetherball is?" Zack asked in disbelief.

"Maybe they don't have it where he comes from," Rick said.

"Well, I'll show you," Zack said.

Peter's eyes darted around nervously. It was obvious he didn't want to play. "Uh, well, I haven't finished unpacking. Marty said we had to finish unpacking before we — "

"What's wrong with you?" Zack asked sharply. "You gonna listen to *everything* your counselor tells you?"

"Well — " Peter stammered.

"Bet I could beat you with one hand behind my back," Zack sneered.

"And on one foot," Dan added.

"Yeah," said Zack. "So how about it, Gummi Bear? Or do we have to start calling you Gummi *Chicken*?"

10

Peter, Zack, Dan, Rick, and I went out to the tetherball court. Lewis, still in the cabin, didn't seem interested in watching the game.

The ball was about the size of a volleyball. It was attached to a rope, and the other end of the rope was attached to the top of a tall metal pole stuck in the ground. The idea was to hit the ball with your fist and make it go around the pole while your opponent tried to make it go in the opposite direction.

Peter and Zack got into position around the tetherball pole.

"You start, Gummi Bear," Zack said, swinging the ball to Peter. Then Zack put his left hand behind his back and raised his left foot off the ground so that he was standing on one foot.

Peter punched the ball. As it swung around the pole, Zack launched himself in the air and belted it with all his might. *Whap!* The ball whipped back around the pole so fast that Peter just barely managed to duck out of the way. As the ball sailed back to Zack, he smacked it again, and then again. The ball rocketed around the pole and reached the end of the tether in no time.

Zack won on one foot with one hand behind his back.

Except for the first time he hit it, Peter never touched the ball again.

Zack grinned triumphantly. Peter trudged into the cabin with his head hanging. Zack had made him look really bad.

"What a dweeb," Dan muttered contemptuously. "And did you see those toenails?"

Zack nodded. "The guy's hopeless." Then he focused on me. "How about *you*, Sleeping Beauty? Think *you* can beat me?"

11

I didn't really want to play Zack and lose. But losing would be better than chickening out. Then again, I didn't want to lose the way Peter lost — never even touching the ball. That wasn't any good either because it would make me look like a wuss. So not only would I have to play, but I'd have to put my body between Zack and the ball, which might cause serious damage to my head.

Given a choice between suffering serious damage to my head or being labeled a chicken wuss, I had to go with the damage.

Taking a deep breath and bracing myself to the prospect of impending pain, I stepped up to the tetherball.

Then I picked up my left leg and put my left arm behind my back. My heart was pounding and my mouth felt dry.

"Whoa!" Rick grinned.

"You don't have to do that," said Zack.

"Hey, I just want to give you an even chance," I replied with a smile.

"All right!" Rick laughed. "This guy's got guts."

"He's still gonna get obliterated," said Dan.

Zack squinted at me, as if wondering if I was really a threat. Then he grinned. "Okay, wise guy, you start."

I steadied the ball with my right hand and prepared to punch it. In my mind was a vision of the ball streaking back at me at supersonic speed and knocking me out cold.

"Hey, guys, time for lunch," someone said. We turned and saw our counselor, Marty, coming toward us. "Where are the others?"

"Still in the cabin," I replied, glad to get out of playing Zack in one-handed, one-footed tetherball.

A few moments later we all started walking toward the dining hall. As I walked with Zack, Rick, and Dan, I noticed that Lewis and Peter followed a dozen yards behind, talking quietly.

What could they be talking about? I wondered. Was Lewis advising Peter to stand up to Zack the way he had?

Meanwhile, the cool guys were also talking quietly.

"You bring the plastic wrap?" Zack asked Dan in a low voice.

41

"Got it right here." Dan patted his pocket. "Who're we gonna do it to?"

"Guess?" Zack jerked his head back toward Peter.

"Who's gonna do it?" Dan asked.

Zack's eyes settled on me. "Sleeping Beauty, who else?"

12

The dining hall was in a big log cabin with a low ceiling. It was noisy and crowded. I spotted Josh and Andy, and we met to compare notes.

"How's your cabin?" I asked Josh.

"Okay," he said with a shrug.

"What about yours?" Andy asked me. "How's it going with the cool guys and Peter the dork?"

"They're really giving him grief," I said.

"You standing up for him?" Andy asked.

"Well, er . . ."

"Forget I even asked." Andy shook his head with disgust. "You're probably too worried about being labeled a dork yourself."

Just then a portly, bald man wearing a gray Camp Walton T-shirt picked up a microphone and told us all to sit. I went back to the table where the guys from B-13 were sitting. The only seat left was next to Peter. Marty sat on Peter's other side and Lewis was sitting across from him.

The portly man's name was Mr. Maller. He was

the owner of the camp. Over the microphone, he told how glad he was that we were all there, how much fun we'd have, and what a big happy family we'd be.

Peter had twisted around in his seat to listen.

Under the table, Zack slipped something into my hand. It was a round piece of plastic wrap.

"Put it over Gummi Bear's glass," he whispered.

It didn't even occur to me to refuse. I reached over and silently stretched the plastic wrap over the top of Peter's glass.

"Make it really smooth so he doesn't notice," Dan added in a hushed voice.

When I was finished, I looked up and straight into the eyes of Lewis, who'd watched the whole thing. I waited for him to say something, or even tell Peter what I'd done. But he just gave me an inscrutable look, and then looked away.

When Mr. Maller's welcoming speech ended, everyone turned back to the table. The camp waiters were coming out of the kitchen with big trays of food. Meanwhile, Zack reached for a metal pitcher in the middle of the table. "Who wants bug juice?"

"Me, me, me, me." Everyone at the table said they wanted some.

"Here you go." Zack stood up and poured out the bug juice. He held the pitcher high so that a long red stream cascaded out and into each glass.

Finally every glass except Peter's was filled.

"So, Gummi Bear, you sure you want some?" Zack asked.

Peter nodded.

"Bombs away." Zack poured.

The red bug juice hit the plastic wrap over Peter's glass and splattered in every direction. Most of it landed on Peter's T-shirt. The rest dripped off the table and into his lap, staining his shorts.

In no time Peter's clothes were drenched in red.

"Gee, how'd that happen?" Zack scratched his head and pretended to be puzzled.

Peter looked down at the plastic-covered glass, and then at Marty, our counselor, sitting on his left. Then he looked at Lewis sitting across from him. Then at me, sitting on his right. We were the closest to him, so it made sense that one of us had put the plastic wrap on his glass.

Obviously Marty wouldn't have done it, and Peter had already made friends with Lewis. Peter's eyes stopped on me, and he stared with a hurt, defeated expression.

He knew I'd done it.

13

Peter went back to the cabin to change his clothes.

Marty gave Zack and Dan a stern look. "Yeah, now I remember. You guys really caused grief in your cabin last year. I'm surprised they let you bunk together again this year."

"Must've been a clerical error," Zack said with a shrug.

"Yeah, right." Marty wasn't fooled. "Try to give Peter a break, okay? You guys can all have a fine time this month without making him miserable, understand?"

We all nodded somberly. But when Marty looked away, Zack cracked a smile and winked.

The waiters served us lunch. Everyone stared down at their plates, but nobody lifted a fork. It was hard to tell exactly what lunch was. It was a glob of red and yellow with bits of green. Looking closely I identified noodles, cheese, and tomato sauce.

"Oh, man, not on the first day," Marty groaned, pressing his face into his hands.

"Yeah, this is no fair," Dan agreed. "They usually wait a few weeks before they hit us with this."

"What is it?" I asked.

"They call it American Chop Suey," Marty said unhappily. "Macaroni and cheese, broccoli, and whatever else happens to be lying around in the kitchen. Then they drown the whole thing in tomato sauce. Don't get the wrong idea, guys. This is a good camp. But the food stinks."

Nobody took more than two bites of the stuff. Lunch became bread, bug juice, and ice cream for dessert. I could have killed Jessica for stealing my donuts.

Afterwards, Marty gave us a tour of the camp, showing us the sports fields, the waterfront, and where the nature walk began. Then we had free time until dinner. Peter and Lewis went their separate ways. I found myself at the basketball court with Rick, Zack, and Dan.

Zack put his hands on his hips and looked around. "Too bad Gummi Bear's not here. It would be kind of fun to play some ball with him. Anyone know where he went?"

"I thought he said something about the nature walk," Rick said.

Zack grinned. "Figures. What about Mighty Mouse?"

"The waterfront," said Dan.

"Why don't the four of us play?" Rick suggested. "We can play two-on-two."

"You play B-ball, Sleeping Beauty?" Zack asked.

"A little," I replied cautiously.

"A little, huh?" Zack said. "Well, then you can be on Rick's team."

So Rick and I teamed up against Dan and Zack to play 21. We played half-court and the game stayed pretty close. Zack was a good basketball player, but Dan wasn't. Rick and I were a more balanced team.

Soon the score was tied 20–20. We were breathing hard. Our wet T-shirts clung to our sweaty bodies and our hair was plastered down with perspiration.

"Next basket wins," Rick reminded us.

Zack paused for a moment and whispered something in Dan's ear.

"Watch out," Rick cautioned me in a low voice. "They're cooking up a plan."

Dan started with the ball and I covered him. Somewhere behind me I could hear the scrape of basketball shoes against the pavement as Zack and Rick jockeyed for position.

Dan drove to my right. As soon as I started to follow, I tripped over something.

The next thing I knew, I was falling.

Wham! I hit the ground, scraping my hands

and knees on the asphalt. Now I knew what had happened. Zack had stuck out his leg so that when Dan started his drive, I'd trip.

Meanwhile Zack spun around and took a pass from Dan. He went in for an easy lay-up and won the game.

"All right!" He and Dan shared a triumphant high five. They were both grinning.

I got up and dusted the dirt off my hands. "Nice trip, Zack."

The smile slowly disappeared from Zack's face. "What'd you say, Sleeping Beauty?"

"You tripped me," I said.

"I did not," Zack said. "You fell."

"Give me a break." I rolled my eyes.

Zack's eyes became beady. "What are you gonna do about it? Go cry to Marty like Gummi Bear would?"

"No," I said.

Zack grinned like he knew he had me, then turned away. It made me mad.

"The cretin says, 'What?' " I muttered in a low voice.

"What?" Zack stopped and looked back at me. The lines between his eyes made a deep V.

Rick grinned. I could see he got it.

"Nothing," I said.

Zack turned away. "Come on, guys," he said to Dan and Rick. "Let's go."

Dan quickly started toward the cabin with

Zack, but Rick stayed behind.

"Hey, come on," he said to me. "It was just a game."

I was still ticked off, but I realized what Rick was doing. He was giving me the chance to keep hanging with the cool guys. I couldn't say no.

14

Everybody met at the cabin before dinner. After the basketball game I was feeling pretty ripe, so I took a shower. When I came out of the bathroom, Zack had taken off his shirt and draped a towel over his shoulder. I figured he was waiting to take a shower next. In the meantime, he was giving Peter grief again.

"You went on the *nature walk*?" Zack made a face. "What are you, some kind of freak?"

Peter bowed his head and stared at the floor.

"Hey, Zack . . ." Rick started to say.

"Yeah, what?" Zack snapped.

"Maybe you should leave the guy alone," Rick said.

"Guy?" Zack stared straight at Peter. "I don't see a guy. I don't know what I see. It's like something from another planet."

Rick didn't answer. For some reason he looked at me.

"The dirtbag says, 'What?' " I muttered.

Zack spun toward me. "What?"

"Shower's free," I said.

Zack forgot about Peter and went into the bathroom. I caught Rick's eye. He winked.

That night after dinner they were showing *Star Wars* in the dining hall. In the cabin before the movie, I saw Zack and Dan talking in low voices and knew they were planning something. Then Dan went into the bathroom.

"Everyone ready?" Marty asked.

"Dan's in the bathroom," Zack said.

"Okay, we'll wait," Marty said.

Dan took forever. After a while, Marty got impatient and walked to the back of the cabin.

"Hey, Dan, you okay?" he called into the bathroom.

"Yeah, I'll be out in a second," Dan called back.

"You sure you're not lost?" Zack yelled and everyone laughed. That was the thing about Zack. Not only was he cool and a good athlete, but he could be funny too.

When he wasn't being mean.

Dan finally got out of the bathroom and we headed toward the dining hall. I was looking forward to sitting with Josh and Andy, but when we got there it was dark inside. The movie had already started.

"Looks like we'll have to sit in the last row," Marty said in a hushed voice.

I had a feeling Zack and Dan had planned it that way. In the meantime, Marty didn't sit down with us.

"Okay, guys, you stay here and watch," he whispered. "I'll be back just before the movie's over." Then he left.

"Where's he going?" I whispered to Rick.

"Probably to hook up with the other counselors and figure out how to meet the counselors from the girls' camp across the lake," Rick whispered back.

We started to watch *Star Wars*, even though you had to assume every camper there had already seen it about a hundred times. After about ten minutes, I felt someone nudge my shoulder. Looking over, I saw Zack, Dan, and Rick sliding out of our row.

"You coming?" Zack whispered.

I hesitated. Marty had told us not to leave the movie.

But if I didn't . . . I was a dweeb.

I didn't ask any questions as we walked through the moonlight back toward the cabin. Crickets chirped in the dark and the night air was fresh and cool. Inside the cabin it was dark, but just enough moonlight came through the windows to allow us to see.

"No lights, guys," Zack whispered, then turned to me. "Hey, Sleeping Beauty, you know how to short-sheet a bed?"

I shook my head.

"Show him, Rick," Zack said as he picked up Peter's Water Pik and shined a small pencil flashlight on it.

Rick pulled the blanket off Peter's bed and started to show me what to do. "See, you double the sheet up short," he said. "Then the guy gets in and can't get his legs straight. We do it to everybody at least once. It's pretty harmless."

"What about Mighty Mouse?" Dan asked.

Zack looked up from the Water Pik and thought for a second. He shook his head. "Let's just do Gummi Bear tonight. Dan, you pull his springs."

While Rick and I doubled over the sheet so that it only went halfway down the bed, Dan crawled underneath. I heard the scrape and squeak of metal as he pulled out some of the springs that supported the mattress. Meanwhile, Zack got a small bottle of liquid detergent and poured it inside the Water Pik.

Dan crawled out from under Peter's bed with a handful of large gray springs. "Man, this is gonna be great! I bet Gummi Bear'll be packed up and gone by the morning."

Rick and I looked at each other. I wondered what he was thinking. Was the point to make Peter so miserable that he'd leave camp?

Rick and I finished. The truth was, I didn't feel good about doing it. Short-sheeting the bed might not be so bad. But the stuff Zack and Dan were doing was mean. Still, I was certain I'd be labeled a geek if I didn't go along with them. And then Zack might start goofing on me, too.

"What else can we do to Gummi Bear?" Dan asked.

Zack started to look around the cabin. But just then Rick walked to the door and peaked out.

"Hey, you hear that?" he whispered to us.

"What?" Zack whispered back.

"I think someone's coming!" Rick hissed.

Everyone froze. Zack tiptoed to the door and looked out. "I don't see anyone," he said in a low voice.

"Well, I thought I saw someone," Rick whispered.

Zack turned back to Dan and me. "Okay, guys, we better get back to the movie."

We quietly snuck out into the dark. No one was outside. I started to wonder if Rick had really seen someone or not. Or was that just his way of stopping Zack and Dan from doing anything more to Peter?

15

We snuck back into the dining hall and watched the end of the movie. Just before the lights went on, Marty rejoined us.

"Okay, guys," he said as the lights went back on, "what do you say we hit the canteen and then head back to the cabin?"

We walked over to the canteen, which was mobbed with campers who had the same idea as us. We got our ice cream, then I spotted Josh and Andy in the crowd and joined them.

"Hey, it's the cool guy," Josh said when he saw me.

"What are you talking about?" I asked.

"We heard about that stunt you pulled on Peter at lunch," Andy said. "You're just too cool for words, Jake."

"Yeah, you're our hero," Josh said snidely.

"Look, forget about it, okay?" I said. "I didn't know he was going to get splattered with bug

56

juice. And anyway, I thought you guys said Peter was a dork."

"Maybe he is," said Andy. "But we wouldn't go out of our way to make his life miserable."

"Not like *someone* we know," added Josh.

"Okay, okay, I get the message," I said. "But how's it going with you guys? Meet anyone in your cabins that you like?"

Andy shrugged his shoulders. "I've spotted a few possible candidates, but I'm taking my time."

"I found a kid in my cabin I like," Josh said. "He's an overweight tubazoid like me. I figure we'll stick together and fight off the cool guys who try to pick on us."

His words stung.

"And speaking of cool guys, how's it going with *you*?" Andy asked.

"All I'm doing is trying to get by, okay?" I said, feeling defensive. "No one wants to be labeled a dork, right?"

"Sure, Jake," Andy said. "Just don't forget, when in doubt, always pick on someone dorkier than you."

I left them and rejoined Marty and the guys, who were walking back to the cabin with their ice creams. Talk about a shock — Zack was having a friendly chat with Peter!

"So, do they call tetherball something else where you come from?" Zack asked.

"Not really," replied Peter. "It never had a name. It was just the game with the ball on the rope. Like soap on a rope."

"Like soap on a rope!" Zack grinned. "That's a good one, Peter."

Peter smiled proudly. He was probably feeling really good because it looked like the cool guys were finally accepting him.

Of course, he didn't know what lay ahead.

16

We got back to the cabin and Marty told us to get ready for bed. Zack had already warned us to stall so that Peter would be the first to use the bathroom.

The rest of us pretended to be busy. Peter was humming to himself, obviously in a good mood. Probably because he thought the cool guys liked him and camp wouldn't be so bad after all. Finally, he got his Water Pik and went into the bathroom. Zack quickly motioned for us to follow.

We couldn't get too close because Peter would see us in the mirror, so we huddled outside the bathroom and listened.

The Water Pik started to whir. Peter was still humming to himself. The humming and whirring sort of mixed together as he started to clean his teeth. But they were quickly joined by a third *spritzing* sound. Like whipped cream squirting out of a can.

"Huh? Wha . . . ?" Peter sounded like he was

trying to talk through a mouthful of food. We heard him spit and gasp, "Hey! What's going on?"

I felt someone prod me from behind. It was Zack, pushing us into the bathroom. Peter saw us in the mirror and spun around. His mouth was covered with foam and it dribbled down his chin. Meanwhile, the Water Pik was spitting out a thin stream of foam over everything in sight!

Zack and Dan started falling all over themselves with laughter. Rick and I were more restrained, but we had to grin. It was a pretty funny sight.

The lines in Peter's forehead deepened as he wiped the foam away from his mouth. His dream of a great month of summer camp was going up in smoke.

Then Marty came into the bathroom. Everyone tensed as we waited to see how he'd react.

When our counselor saw what happened he just shook his head and smiled. "Don't worry, Peter. It's a practical joke. We always get them on the first day. But that's the end of it, right, Zack?"

"Sure, dude, we were just fooling around." Zack patted Peter on the back. A small smile appeared on Peter's face as he tried to laugh along with everyone else. Meanwhile, Marty turned to Zack. "Okay, guys, enough funny stuff. Let's get to bed."

We drifted back to our bunks. Peter stayed in the bathroom to rinse the detergent out of the

Water Pik. Then he came out. We all watched as he pulled back his blanket and hopped into bed.

Ripppp! Peter's eyes went wide and his jaw dropped. With those long toenails, his feet must've torn right through the sheet!

Creak! Before he had time to react, the bottom of the bed parted where Dan had pulled out the springs.

Thwamp! Peter and his mattress sank through the opening and settled on the floor.

"Hey!" Peter struggled to get out of the bed. The mattress had closed around him like a glove. His arms and legs waved wildly like a beetle who'd been turned upside down. No matter how hard he tried, he couldn't get enough of a grip to lift himself out.

Meanwhile, Dan and Zack were doubled over with laughter. But this time, Marty didn't smile as he helped Peter out of his bed. As soon as Peter was on his feet, he bolted out the screen door and disappeared outside.

Marty glared at us angrily, then followed Peter into the dark.

17

We waited around in the cabin for Marty and Peter to come back. Dan chewed nervously on his fingernails and toyed with his diamond stud earring.

"Maybe we went too far, Zack," he said.

Zack smirked and pushed his fingers through his bushy blond hair. "What can they do? Throw all four of us out of camp on the first day? Forget it. Our parents would all ask for refunds. Old Man Maller's too tight to give back a cent."

"You think Peter'll come back?" Rick asked.

"I hope not," Zack said. "You really want a geek like that in our cabin?"

Rick and I exchanged another look. I got the feeling he didn't feel any better about what just happened than I did. But if we both felt that way, how come we couldn't stand up to Zack and tell him to lay off Peter?

We waited. The only sound in the cabin was

that kid Lewis, lying on the bunk above Peter's, slowly thumbing through a car magazine.

After a while, Marty came back. The corners of his mouth curled down. "Congratulations, guys, you've probably ruined Peter's summer."

"It was just a joke," Zack said with a shrug.

"No, it wasn't *just* a joke," Marty replied angrily. "It was too many jokes and all aimed at the same kid. After a while it changes from a joke to a message. And Peter heard it loud and clear."

"So where is he?" Rick asked.

"He's staying in another cabin tonight," Marty said. "Right now he's determined to leave camp tomorrow. I'm going to see if I can talk him out of it, but I have my doubts." He leveled his gaze at Zack. "Congratulations on a job well done, jerk."

Zack shrugged. Marty got some things out of Peter's cubby.

"I'm going to bring him his stuff," he said. "It's way past lights out, so just go to bed. Last guy turns off the lights."

Marty left the cabin again.

"Man, what a dork," Zack muttered.

"Yeah," Dan agreed.

I washed up and climbed into my bunk. The camp pillow was hard and lumpy, and the blanket itched. A few moments later, Rick turned off the lights and walked with his flashlight to the bunk under mine.

I lay in the dark feeling really bad. It looked like I'd managed to get in with the cool guys. But in doing so, I'd helped ruin Peter Peeling's summer. And he'd done nothing to deserve it. It wasn't his fault that he was dorky, or that he had an overprotective mother.

I yawned and felt myself growing sleepy. My first day of camp was over. But I knew that if I had it to do all over again, I would do it differently.

18

DAY TWO

The bus went over a bump and I felt my eyes open. Wha . . . ? Where was I?

On a bus?

How?

I sat up straight and looked out the window. The bus was pulling into a big gravel parking lot. Other buses were already there and kids wearing white Camp Walton shirts were climbing out of them.

Wait a minute! I felt a shock race through me. Like being zapped with a cattle prod.

It was the same as yesterday.

Like, been there, done that!

What was going on? Was this a dream?

I sure hoped it was.

I looked a few rows ahead and saw the back of Peter Peeling's head. In the row in front of him, Josh and Andy were getting their things together.

I twisted around. In the back seat, Zack, Dan, and Rick were getting up.

It definitely felt more real than a dream.

"Have a nice nap, Sleeping Beauty?" Zack asked with a grin.

Oh no! This was sounding totally *too* familiar.

"What's the matter?" Zack asked me. "Can't talk?"

"I can talk," I said.

"Good, we were worried there for a moment." Zack smiled as he, Dan, and Rick filed down the aisle past me.

"See ya in the cabin," said Rick.

I watched them go down the aisle. Meanwhile, Peter stood up, clutching his white shopping bag.

"Cool bag," said Zack with a chuckle.

Same as yesterday . . .

I was stuck in the first day of camp!

19

Why me?
     I took a deep breath and let it out slowly. Well, maybe I shouldn't have been so surprised.

The reason I wasn't totally instantly freaked out of my skull was that this wasn't the first time it had happened. Last time I'd gotten stuck in the first day of school.

The difference between last time and this time was simple. Last time I didn't know why I'd been stuck in the same day over and over again. This time it was obvious.

Whoever was in charge of these things decided I was going to do the first day over again.

Because of Peter.

In a strange way I was sort of glad, because this time I'd do it right.

I grabbed my day pack and started down the aisle, but when I got to Peter's seat, I stopped.

"Have a good ride?" I asked him. Meanwhile, in

the seat in front of Peter, Andy and Josh swiveled around and watched.

Peter gave me an uncertain look. "Uh, it was okay, I guess."

"I fell asleep," I said. "Was it a long trip?"

"Just a couple of hours," Peter said. "Not too bad."

"Well, come on," I said, hitching my day pack over my shoulder. "We better get off."

"Uh, yeah." If Peter was acting a little wary, it was probably because I'd acted like I didn't want to sit with him before. Of course I couldn't explain why. The only thing I could do was be really friendly now.

Peter and I got off the bus, followed by Josh and Andy. Outside, the driver was pulling the duffle bags out of the luggage carrier. Rick, Dan, and Zack were waiting for theirs.

"There's my duffle," Peter said, and went to get it. That's when I felt a tap on my shoulder. Wheeling around, I found Josh and Andy behind me.

"What's with you?" Josh asked in a low voice.

"What are you talking about?" I played dumb.

"When you got on the bus you acted like you didn't want to sit next to that Peeling kid," Andy said. "Now you're acting like best friends. So, what gives?"

"The reason I didn't sit with him was because

I knew I was gonna sleep," I lied. "I mean, forget what he looks like. The guy's in my cabin and I'm gonna be friendly with him no matter what."

Josh and Andy shared a funny look, but didn't say anything more about it. By then Peter had gotten his duffle bag and was headed toward our cabin.

"I guess our cabins will be up that way, too," Josh said.

"No, you guys are over there." I pointed toward the cabins on the other side of the athletic field.

Andy frowned. "How do you know that?"

"It's weird," I said with a shrug. "I just feel like I've been here before."

I saw the driver pull out my duffle bag and drop it to the ground with a thud near where Zack, Dan, and Rick were standing. I went over and struggled to pick it up.

Dan started to smile.

"No, it's not bowling balls," I said.

He scowled.

By now, Andy and Josh had gotten their duffle bags and spoke to the guy with the clipboard.

Andy turned and looked at me with a puzzled expression. "You were right. Our cabins are over there. How'd you know?"

I was going to explain how I'd seen it all in my crystal ball. But out of the corner of my eye I saw

Peter's white shopping bag split and all his stuff spill out onto the ground.

The cool guys were going to catch up to him any second. I quickly turned back to Andy and Josh.

"Gotta run, dudes," I said.

20

Peter put down his duffle and started to pick up his stuff, including the Water Pik.

"Hey, guys, look," Zack was saying as I caught up to them. "A Water Pik."

"Whoa." Dan grinned. "This guy takes serious care of his teeth."

"It's for my gums," Peter tried to explain.

"Gums, huh?" chuckled Dan. "Hey, maybe we should call him Gummi Bear."

"Yeah, and maybe we should call you Gummi *Brains*," I said.

The cool guys spun around and stared at me. I felt weird. Like in that instant I had just become their enemy.

"Well, look who's here. It's Sleeping Beauty," Zack said. He nudged Dan. "You gonna take that from him?"

Dan narrowed his eyes at me. He was shorter than me, but more powerfully built. I felt my stomach tighten. I didn't want to fight, but I might not have a choice.

"Didn't you say you were in B-13?" Dan asked.

"That's right."

"Better learn to sleep with one eye open," he warned me, then turned to the others. "Come on, guys, let's let these two geeks get to know each other."

Zack and Dan started toward the cabin. Rick gave me a puzzled look, and then followed. I kneeled down with Peter and helped him pick up his stuff.

"Thanks, Jake," he said.

"Hey, always available to help pick stuff up," I said with a grin.

"That's not what I meant," Peter said.

"I know." I winked at him.

Between the two of us, we managed to pick up all his stuff.

"Maybe we'll get lucky and they'll leave us alone," Peter said under his breath as we walked toward the cabin.

"Yeah." I pretended to agree. But knowing Zack, we were going to be anything *but* lucky.

21

We got into the cabin. The cool guys had already staked out the bunks in the back.

Thunk! I dropped my duffle bag next to the first double decker. Standing by his bunk in the back, Zack leveled his gaze at me. I knew what he was going to say.

"It never fails, right?" I said.

Zack blinked as if I'd taken the words out of his mouth.

Peter came in and dropped his duffle bag next to mine. "What never fails?" he asked me in a low voice.

"The jerks take the bunks in the back," I whispered.

Peter grinned.

Just like the day before, Lewis was the last kid in the cabin. This time the only bed left was the top of Rick's double decker.

"Looks like we've got ourselves a real winner cabin this year," Zack muttered.

"Yeah, I wonder if it's too late to get a transfer," Dan replied.

I could have said something, but I decided to keep my mouth shut. There was no sense in asking for trouble. I was pretty sure I was going to have enough of it anyway.

A little later Marty came in and told us all to introduce ourselves. I turned to Peter and told him to come with me.

"Why?" he asked when he saw that I was heading toward the back of the cabin.

"You'll see," I said.

Peter reluctantly followed me. I stopped next to Zack's bunk.

"Listen, Zack," I said. "This is Peter Peeling. And that's what he wants to be called, not Gummi Bear. Our parents were friends when we were little. I haven't seen him in a long time, but he's a good guy."

Zack gave me a blank look. Then a slight smile crept onto his lips. "He can't introduce himself?"

"Well, you guys gave him a pretty hard time before," I said.

"What are you, his bodyguard?" Dan sneered.

"Look, we don't all have to be friends, okay?" I said. "But we do have to live together in this cabin. Now we can either have a good time or a miserable time. It's up to you."

Zack nodded slowly. "Thanks for telling me

that, Sleeping Beauty." Then he offered his hand to Peter. "I'm Zack Zanko."

"Uh, hi," Peter replied and shook his hand.

For a split second I felt pretty good. Like maybe things would work out after all. But then Peter's face turned pale and he started to wince. I looked down at their hands. Zack was squeezing so hard his knuckles had turned white.

"Nice to meet you, Peter," Zack said with an icy grin.

22

After Zack let go of Peter's hand, we went back to unpacking. Marty left for the waterfront and Zack looked up at Lewis, who was kneeling on his bunk, tacking up his car pictures.

"Guess you're into cars, huh?" Zack asked.

Lewis nodded.

"*Small* cars, right?" Zack said.

"*Fast* cars," Lewis replied.

"*Small* fast cars, then," said Zack with a grin.

In the back of the cabin Dan snickered. Hearing it again really made me mad.

"The jerk-magnet says 'What?' " I said in a low voice.

Zack turned and frowned. "What?"

Rick smiled.

"Why do you have to pick on everybody?" I asked Zack.

This time Zack didn't look surprised that I'd interfered. "I wasn't talking to *you*, Sleeping Beauty."

"Well, I'm talking to you," I said, facing him.

"Hey," Lewis said from up on his bunk. Zack and I both looked up at him. Lewis was looking at me. "Thanks, but I can take care of myself."

"Whoa!" Dan chuckled. "Sounds like we got a whole *cabin* full of tough guys."

"Yeah." Zack cracked his knuckles. "Maybe it's time to find out just how tough everyone *really* is."

"Hey, who wants to play that new tetherball game?" Rick suddenly asked.

Zack looked around. "Yeah, sure, let's play." He turned to Peter. "Wanna play some tetherball, Gummi Bear?"

"Uh, I'm not sure," Peter replied nervously.

Zack put his hands on his hips. "What are you, some kind of wuss?"

"No, he's not a wuss," I said. "Not only that, but he'll play you on one foot and with one hand behind his back."

"I will?" Peter asked, bewildered.

Zack scowled, then grinned. "That's just what I was gonna say. Okay, let's do it!"

He, Dan, and Rick went outside. Peter hesitated and looked at me. "What's tetherball?"

"It's the game with the pole and the ball on the rope," I said. "Don't worry, you can do it."

Peter's eyes darted around nervously. "But I haven't finished unpacking. Marty said we had to finish unpacking before we — "

"Yeah, I know," I said. "But if you don't go out there and play, Zack is going to give you grief forever. You can finish unpacking later."

Peter winced at the thought of facing Zack in tetherball.

"Go on, Peter," I urged him. "You don't have to beat him, just go out there and show that you're willing to play."

"Aren't you coming?" Peter asked.

"Sure," I said. "I'll be out in a second."

"Promise?" Peter asked.

"Yeah, honest, I promise."

Peter went out the screen door. I looked up at Lewis, who was still tacking car pictures to the rafters.

"Hey, Lewis?" I said.

"Yeah." He paused and looked down at me.

"About what happened before," I said. "The only reason I spoke up against Zack is because I think you, me, and Peter better stick together, okay?"

"Why?" Lewis asked.

"Because I have a feeling those guys are gonna cause a lot of trouble for us," I said.

Lewis gazed past me. It seemed like he was looking out the screen door at the cool guys, who were getting ready to play tetherball. "Thanks, Jake. But like I said before, I can take care of myself."

I left the cabin. Zack, Dan, and Rick were standing by the tetherball court with Peter. Zack was already on one foot, waiting while Peter tried to decide which foot and hand to use. The poor guy was totally uncoordinated. Zack was going to demolish him.

"Hey, wait a minute," I said. "This isn't really fair."

Zack rolled his eyes. "Now what?"

"Well, tetherball is something you're really good at," I said. "So of course you're gonna beat Peter. If he has to play you in tetherball, then you should agree to play him at something he's really good at."

"Okay, sure," Zack said with a sigh. "What'll it be, Gummi Bear?"

"Uh . . ." Peter had to think. "How about Scrabble?"

"*Scrabble?*" Zack repeated in disbelief. Dan clamped his hand over his mouth to keep from laughing out loud. Even I had to admit it wasn't the best idea.

"Isn't there something else?" I asked Peter. "You know, something you guys can play *outside*?"

Peter bit his lip. "Croquet?"

"You mean, with the wooden balls and the mallets and the wire thingies?" Dan asked.

"They're called wickets," Peter informed him.

"Oh, man." Zack shook his head and groaned. "What a dork!"

Peter gave me a pleading look, like he hoped I'd come to his rescue. I really wanted to, but it wasn't going to be easy.

23

Fortunately, before Zack had a chance to slaughter Peter in one-handed tetherball, Marty arrived and took us to lunch. The cool guys went ahead and Peter and I followed.

"Just my luck," Peter muttered under his breath.

"What do you mean?" I asked.

"I have to get stuck in a cabin with those guys," he said.

"I have a feeling there might be guys like that in *any* cabin," I said.

Peter nodded. "Well, then I guess I'm lucky that we're in this together."

Maybe, I thought.

Once again the dining hall was noisy and crowded with kids. I saw Josh and Andy.

"Catch you later," I said to Peter, planning to go talk to my friends.

"Where're you going?" he asked.

"Uh, just to talk to my friends," I said.

Peter glanced at the table where B-13 sat. The cool guys were already there. He turned to me. "Uh, can I come with you?"

"Hey, don't worry," I said. "I'll be back in a minute."

Peter didn't look happy, but he headed toward the table while I headed toward my friends.

"How's it going with the cool guys and Peter the dork?" Andy asked.

"They're really giving him grief," I said.

"You standing up for him?" Andy asked.

"Better believe it."

Andy and Josh traded an uncertain look.

"You sure that's what you want to do?" Josh asked.

"Hey, someone's got to do it," I said. "Otherwise, the kid's gonna be this summer's sacrificial lamb."

"Yeah, but how about *you*?" Andy asked.

"What about me?" I asked, not understanding what he meant.

"How are you gonna have any fun if you're always defending Peter?" he asked.

Out of the corner of my eye, I saw Mr. Maller, the owner of the camp, walking toward the microphone. I knew I wouldn't have time to explain to my friends that I was trapped in the first day of camp, and that I was pretty certain that the only way I could get out of it was by defending Peter.

"Hey, look, guys," I said. "I'm just trying to do the right thing."

Josh was just about to say something when Mr. Maller got on the microphone and started his speech about how glad he was that we were all there, how much fun we'd have, and what a big happy family we'd be. I said good-bye to my friends, and went back to our table. I sat next to Peter, who had twisted around in his seat to listen to Mr. Maller. Zack and Dan were giving each other looks. Little did they know that I knew what they were planning.

24

Mr. Maller's speech ended, and everyone turned back to the table. The camp waiters were coming out of the kitchen with the trays of American Chop Suey. Zack started to reach for the metal pitcher in the middle of the table, but I grabbed it first and stood up. "Who wants bug juice?"

"Me," Peter said.

I looked down at his glass. It was covered with the plastic wrap. "Oh, gee, your glass has something on it."

Peter stared down at his glass, then removed the plastic wrap. I poured the bright red bug juice.

"Anyone else?" I asked, turning toward the cool guys.

Zack was sitting with his arms crossed, glowering at me. He was obviously mad that I'd foiled his trick.

"I'll have some." Dan held up his glass.

With the pitcher in my hand, I stretched across the table toward him. Unfortunately, I *missed!*

Bright red bug juice splashed all over the table in front of Dan and onto his shirt.

"Hey! What're you doing!" Dan yelled and jumped up.

"Oh, gee, I'm really sorry," I pretended to gasp.

Meanwhile, Zack started to laugh . . . until I *accidentally* spilled bug juice on him too.

"You idiot!" Zack shouted and jumped up. His shirt had a big red stain on it.

"Sorry," I apologized.

"No, you're not!" Zack growled, making a fist. "You did it on purpose!"

The next thing I knew, he started around the table toward me with both hands balled into fists. Luckily for me, Marty got up and blocked his path.

"Chill out, Zack," our counselor said. "Jake said it was an accident."

"Bull," Zack sputtered. "He knew exactly what he was doing. He did it because of the plastic wrap on Gummi Bear's glass. He — "

"That reminds me," Marty said. "Just *how* did the plastic wrap get on Peter's glass?"

Zack suddenly quieted down. He glared past Marty at me. "You're dead meat, Sleeping Beauty."

"Ooh, I'm really scared," I replied.

"Both of you, knock it off," Marty ordered.

"Zack and Dan, go back to the cabin and put on dry clothes. Jake, you promise to be more careful pouring the bug juice next time?"

"You bet." I nodded.

Zack and Dan left. The waiters served lunch and once again we stared at the American Chop Suey in disbelief. I figured the bug juice incident was behind us, so I was surprised when Marty looked up from his plate and said, "Hey, Jake, *did* you do it on purpose?"

"Uh . . ." I didn't know what to say.

"Tell the truth," our counselor said.

"Okay, yeah, I did," I answered.

"Why?" Marty asked.

"Because I don't like the way they pick on Peter," I said.

Marty nodded as if he understood. "No more of that."

25

After lunch, Marty gave us the tour of the camp and then told us we had free time until dinner. I suggested to Peter that we do something together.

"Like what?" he asked.

"I don't know," I said as I watched Rick, Zack, and Dan head for the basketball court. "What do you want to do?"

"Well . . ." Peter scratched his head. "You want to play Scrabble?"

Playing Scrabble was close to the last thing in the world I wanted to do. "Hey, look," I said. "It's a beautiful day. Why don't we do something outside?"

"We could play Scrabble outside," Peter said.

I couldn't help but sigh. I had made it my sworn duty to protect Peter from the cool guys, and make sure he had a decent time at camp. It was the right thing to do. Besides, if I didn't I'd probably be trapped in the first day of camp forever. And if I had to look at American Chop Suey one more time, I was going to barf.

But it wasn't going to be easy to help Peter. The absolute last thing I wanted to do was play Scrabble *outside*. If anyone saw us we'd be labeled super-mega-*quadra*-dorks.

"I really think we should save Scrabble for a rainy day," I said. "Isn't there anything else you'd like to do?"

"Uh . . ." Peter rubbed his chin. "That nature walk sounds pretty interesting."

The nature walk!? Inwardly I groaned. But at least we'd be outside. Besides, I probably wouldn't have to worry about running into anyone I knew. The only guys we'd meet on the nature walk were bound to be dorks.

26

"What happened to you?" Josh asked when I saw him and Andy outside the dining hall before dinner that night.

"Peter wanted to go on a nature walk," I said, scratching my arm.

"A nature walk?" Andy made a face.

"Hey, it was an educational experience," I said, scratching my ear. "I learned about three different kinds of butterflies, two different kinds of skunk cabbage, a painted turtle, and a red-winged bluebird."

"*Black*bird," Josh corrected me.

"Whatever," I said with a shrug.

Andy studied my face. "I count seven mosquito bites on the left side of your forehead alone."

"The grand body total's somewhere around sixty," I said, scratching my neck. My head, neck, and arms were covered with itching red welts. The nature walk had led Peter and me through a mosquito-infested swamp.

89

Josh shook his head. "Look, I know you're trying to be a nice guy, Jake. But maybe you ought to spend a little less time with Peter. Not just because everyone's going to think of you as a dork by association, but it's also hazardous to your health."

"I can't," I said.

"Why not?"

I looked around to make sure no one else was listening. Then in a low voice I said, "Because I'm trapped in the first day of camp."

"You're *what?*" Josh's forehead wrinkled.

"I'm trapped in the first day of camp," I said. "Today's the first day of camp for *you*, but for me, yesterday was."

"Yesterday we were back in Jeffersonville," Andy said. "We went Rollerblading, remember?"

"*You* did," I said. "I was here at camp."

"No, you weren't," Josh said. "You were with us."

I shook my head. "Listen, I know this is really hard to explain, but this is the *second* time I've been through this day. Yesterday when we got to camp I tried to be one of the cool guys. I picked on Peter. That was the wrong thing to do so I got punished. They're making me do the day over again."

"Who's making you do it over?" Andy asked.

"I don't know who," I said. "But it's happened to me before. Remember the first day of school last year when Alex Silver decided to be the Knight of Wedgy and wedgy everyone?"

"Oh, yeah." Andy grinned at the memory. "He thought he was so totally cool."

"Well, originally I was into it too," I said. "We were the Knights of Wedgy together. I mean, you have to admit that it feels good to be in with the cool guys."

Andy and Josh both nodded.

"But the thing is," I went on. "If you have to pick on kids to prove you're cool, are you *really* cool? Or are you just some jerk who has to scare kids into thinking he's cool?"

Josh made a funny face. "What does this have to do with going through the first day of camp over again?"

"I had to do the first day of school over about six times before I figured out that being nice to people is better than being mean and cool," I explained. "So now that I'm stuck in the first day of camp I know I have to be really nice to Peter and protect him from the cool guys. Once I've done that, I'll be able to get to the second day of camp."

Josh and Andy shared another doubtful glance.

Then Josh cleared his throat. "I hate to say this, Jake, but are you aware of the fact that you've totally wigged out?"

"Look, it's dumb to argue about this," I said. "You'll never believe me. I probably shouldn't have told you. The weird thing is that it doesn't actually matter. After today everything's going to be normal anyway."

"Except that you and Peter the Geek are joined at the hip," Andy pointed out.

"If Jake really believes this stuff about being trapped in the first day of camp, maybe he *should* be joined with Peter at the hip," Josh said.

"You mean, like two peas in a pod?" Andy asked.

"More like two nuts in a shell," Josh said.

I just smiled. "Whatever you say, guys."

27

After dinner was the movie. I sat on the bench in the back of the dining hall with Peter and the other guys from our cabin. As soon as the movie started, Marty warned us not to get into any trouble, and left. Then the cool guys left.

"Where're they going?" Peter whispered to me.

"Back to the cabin," I whispered back.

"Why?"

"To set booby traps for us."

In the dark, Peter frowned. "How do you know?"

"Trust me," I said in a low voice. "Now listen, I'm gonna leave too. If I don't get back here before the movie ends, tell Marty I had a bad stomachache and went to the nurse."

"Where are you really going?" Peter whispered back.

"I'm going to take care of a few things," I said and started to slide down the bench. Then I stopped and turned back to Peter.

"One last thing," I said. "After the movie you're gonna go get ice cream and Zack's gonna start acting really friendly to you."

"Why?" Peter asked.

"Because he wants to set you up," I explained. "He wants you to think he's going to be your pal so that you won't expect the booby traps. Anyway, when he does it, act like you think he's sincere."

"Why?" Peter asked.

"Because that's how we'll set *him* up," I replied with a wink.

I left the dining hall. Outside the crickets were chirping in the moonlight. Up ahead I could see Zack and his buddies walking quickly back to the cabin. That's where I was headed too, but instead of following them, I snuck around the back of the cabins until I got to B-13.

Standing on my tiptoes behind the cabin I was able to peek in through the screened bathroom window. The cabin was dark and I couldn't see much, but I could hear whispers and the squeak of bedsprings as the cool guys set their traps.

Little did they know that I had a few booby traps of my own to set.

Leaving the back of the cabin, I snuck around the side and found the hose. I brought it around to the front of the cabin and left the nozzle next to the big patch of dirt at the bottom of the front steps. I let the water run slowly and quietly, creating a big mud puddle.

Next I borrowed the clothesline and tied it across the bottom step to the porch, about eight inches from the floor. In the dark, the cool guys would never see it.

Now it was time to sit back and wait.

About fifteen minutes later, the front door of the cabin creaked open and Zack came out, followed by Dan and Rick. Crouching around the side of the cabin, I peeked up and watched.

"Okay, dudes," Zack said as he crossed the porch and started down the front steps. "Let's get back to the . . . *Ahhh!*"

He tripped over the clothesline.

Ker-splat!

Zack fell face-first into the mud puddle.

Up on the porch, Dan looked shocked. Rick had a slight grin on his face. I was starting to wonder whose side that guy was really on.

"What the . . . ?" Zack jumped to his feet in the middle of the puddle. The whole front half of his body was soaked brown with mud. It was in his hair and on his face. His arms and legs were covered.

"Hey, check this out." Dan pointed at the clothesline tied across the bottom step. "Looks like someone booby trapped us while we were booby trapping Gummi Bear."

Zack looked around, fuming. "I bet I know who it was, too."

"So what are you gonna do?" Dan asked.

"I'm gonna take a shower and change my clothes," Zack said. "Then I'm gonna find Sleeping Beauty and destroy him."

28

Rick and Dan headed back to the dining hall. Zack went back into the cabin to change his clothes and clean up. As soon as I heard the shower start to run, I snuck in. The cabin was dark. Only the bathroom light was on. Picking my way around the bunks, I quietly found the pen light in Zack's cubby. Holding the light between my teeth, I pulled every pair of pants and shorts out of his cubby. Then I snuck back out and hid them under the porch.

A couple of minutes later the shower stopped. Zack muttered angrily to himself as he toweled off. He kept grumbling about how he was going to break my skull and make me eat mud. He left the bathroom and headed back to his bunk to put on clean clothes.

"Huh? What the???"

He'd just discovered that he had no pants or shorts. "Oh, man, I'll kill that kid," he muttered.

"Just wait till I find him. I'm gonna break both of his arms."

A few moments later the door of the cabin swung open and slammed closed. From around the corner of the cabin I watched Zack head back toward the dining hall wearing a pair of Dan's shorts all bunched up at the waist.

There was still work to do. Luckily, I had time because the guys were going to go for ice cream after the movie.

I went back into the cabin and found the springs Dan had taken from Peter's and my double-decker bunk. After putting them back where they belonged, I unshort-sheeted our beds and rinsed the detergent out of Peter's Water Pik.

Now it was time to get to work on Zack and Dan's bunk.

29

I was lying on my bed when the cabin door creaked open and Marty came in, followed by the rest of the guys.

"What happened to you?" Marty asked.

"I had a stomachache and went to see the nurse," I said. "I just got back here a few minutes ago."

"Does it still hurt?" he asked.

"Naw, it's a lot better," I said.

Marty told the rest of the guys to get ready for bed. When Zack passed my bunk, he squinted angrily to let me know that I hadn't fooled him. I smiled back.

Just like the night before, the cool guys stalled and pretended to be busy so that Peter would be the first to use the bathroom. Finally, Peter got his Water Pik and went into the bathroom humming to himself. I'd warned him about what was going to happen, so he knew he had to pretend to be in a good mood and act like he thought the cool guys liked him.

As soon as Peter went into the bathroom, Zack quickly motioned for the cool guys to follow. They huddled outside the doorway and listened.

The Water Pik started to whir. Peter was still humming to himself. The humming and whirring mixed together as he started to clean his teeth.

And that's the way it stayed until Peter finished.

Frowning, Zack turned away from the bathroom entrance. Once again, he looked up at me on my bunk and narrowed his eyes. He must've realized that I'd undone his booby traps.

The rest of the guys brushed their teeth and washed up. Then Zack climbed up to his bunk. At the same time, Dan pulled back his blanket and started to get in the bed below.

Sploosh!

Rip!

Zack's mouth fell open. I'd not only short-sheeted his and Dan's beds, I'd added a few water balloons for good measure. He'd not only torn through his sheets, but soaked his mattress as well.

Zack stared daggers at me. "Why you!"

He jumped out of bed, but Marty stepped into his path.

"What's the matter, Zack?" our counselor asked with a smile. "Can't take a joke?"

Zack was seething, balling and unballing his fists, his face red with fury. He just glared past Marty at me and didn't reply.

Dan and Zack went to get new sheets. While they were out Marty talked to me.

"Listen, Jake," he said, barely able to hide his smile. "Let's not have any more of that kind of stuff, okay?"

I nodded, but really got the feeling our counselor was glad that Zack had gotten what he deserved. Peter winked at me and smiled. Lewis looked sort of amused. Rick listened and watched, but said nothing. Still, he didn't look annoyed or anything.

Zack and Dan came back with some towels and dry sheets. They spread the towels over the wet spots on their mattresses, then made their beds with the new sheets and got in.

"Oh, man," Dan moaned. "The water still seeps through."

Zack didn't say anything, but I imagined the water had seeped through his sheets, too.

Marty turned off the cabin lights and told us to go to sleep. I lay in bed in the dark. Despite that hard, lumpy pillow and itchy blanket, I felt pretty good. I'd done the right thing this time. Hopefully with my help, Peter would have a half-decent summer.

And I would get out of being trapped in the first day of camp.

I was just falling asleep when I heard the faintest whisper come from the direction of Zack's bunk. "Hey, Sleeping Beauty."

"What?" I whispered back.

"You better get a good night's rest," Zack whispered. "Because tomorrow you're dead meat."

I rolled over and pulled my pillow over my head so I wouldn't have to listen to any more of his threats.

But it made me wonder.

Maybe I'd made things better for Peter. But I'd also made them pretty bad for me.

Was that the way it *had* to be?

30

DAY THREE

I felt a bump and opened my eyes. Huh? What was I doing on the bus?

It must have been a dream.

I closed my eyes.

Then opened them again.

I was still on the bus.

And it didn't feel like a dream.

This was weird.

Because it *had* to be a dream.

I sat up and looked out the window. We were pulling into the parking lot. The other buses were already there and the new campers wearing white Camp Walton T-shirts were climbing out.

Next I looked inside the bus. Peter was in his seat a few rows ahead. In the row in front of him, Josh was taking off his headphones, and Andy was closing his magazine.

I twisted around. In the backseat, Zack, Dan, and Rick were getting up.

"Have a nice nap, Sleeping Beauty?" Zack asked with a grin.

Uh-oh!

This was no dream!

It was happening again! But why? How was it possible? *I'd done the right thing the day before!*

"What's the matter?" Zack asked. "Can't talk?"

"Uh . . ." I didn't know what to say. I didn't know what to do. I was trapped in the first day of camp again. But it didn't make sense. Hadn't I done what I was supposed to do to get out of this mess?

Why hadn't it worked?

Zack raised an eyebrow. "Is 'uh' all you can say?"

He was waiting for me to say something, but I didn't know what to do. If being friendly didn't work, and being *unfriendly* was no good either, then what was the answer?

I looked up into Zack's face as he, Dan, and Rick filed down the aisle past me. Zack's mouth was a hard, straight line. Dan gave me a curious look.

I stretched and yawned.

"See ya in the cabin," said Rick.

They passed Peter as he stood up with his white paper shopping bag. Zack made his comment about the bag, and Dan chuckled. Once again, Peter looked away and waited until they left the bus. Then he went down the aisle and got off.

And that left Josh, Andy, and me on the bus. I knew Josh would ask why I didn't sit with them, and Andy would accuse me of not wanting to sit with Peter because I wanted to make friends with the cool guys.

"You're right," I said before either of them had a chance to speak. "I didn't feel like sitting with Peter. But I didn't make friends with the cool guys either. And I don't think I'm going to."

Josh blinked with surprise. "How'd you know I was gonna ask about that?"

"Because that's what you asked me yesterday," I said.

"What are you talking about?" he said. "How could I have asked that yesterday?"

"Because we were all on this bus and you asked me why I didn't want to sit with you," I explained.

Andy and Josh shared a bewildered look.

"I've got news for you, Jake," Andy said. "You weren't here yesterday. Today's the first day of camp."

"It is for you guys," I said. "But it's the third day for me. Actually, it's my first day for the third time."

Josh and Andy traded really worried looks.

"Are you feeling okay?" Josh asked me.

"No, I'm totally freaked," I said. "This is the third time I've stood on this bus and talked to you like this. And for all I know I may be doing it for the rest of my life."

"Maybe you need to get some more sleep," Andy said, a little nervously.

"No, guys, I'm telling you the truth," I said. Then I explained how I was trapped in the first day of camp, just like I'd once been trapped in the first day of school.

Neither of my friends said a word when I was done. I could tell from their expressions that they thought I was completely insane.

"Listen, guys, I really need you to believe me," I said desperately. "When I was stuck in the first day of school I got out of it by doing the right thing. But I did the right thing yesterday and I'm still trapped."

"I think the right thing for you would be to spend the summer in a mental institution," Josh said.

"I'm not joking, guys," I said.

"Uh, boys?" Down at the front of the bus Mr. Maller had climbed back on. "Time to get off and get your bags."

"We're coming, Mr. Maller," I said.

The camp owner got off the bus.

"Who's he?" Andy asked.

"He owns the camp," I said.

"How do *you* know?" Josh asked.

"I *told* you. I've been here for three days."

Josh rolled his eyes in disbelief.

"Uh, I think we better get off," Andy said.

We started down the aisle toward the front of the bus.

"Guys," I whispered. "For the last time, you have to help me. I don't know what to do."

"It's simple, Jake," Josh whispered back. "You get off the bus. You weren't here yesterday. You were back in Jeffersonville. We spent the day Rollerblading, remember?"

"*You* guys did," I said. "Not me. I spent the day protecting Peter from the cool guys."

"Sure, Jake, whatever you say," Andy whispered.

31

We got off the bus. The driver was pulling the duffle bags out of the luggage carrier. Rick, Dan, and Zack were waiting for theirs. Peter got his duffle bag and headed toward our cabin.

Josh started to say something.

"Your cabins are over there." I pointed toward the cabins on the other side of the athletic field.

"How do you know?" Andy asked.

"I *told* you," I said wearily. "I've already been here, done this."

"We better check with a counselor just to make sure," Josh said, clearly not trusting me.

"Thanks for believing me, guys," I grumbled bitterly.

Josh had a pained expression on his face. "How are we supposed to believe that you were here yesterday when we were with you back in Jeffersonville?"

I was tired of trying to explain it. Maybe I was expecting too much from my friends. I mean, even I found it hard to believe. And I was *living* it!

I left Josh and Andy, and went to get my duffle bag. Dan started to smile. I knew what he was going to ask, of course.

"Grenades, land mines, and mortar shells," I said. "I'm a very violent person."

He scowled.

Andy and Josh got their duffle bags and spoke to the guy with the clipboard, who pointed toward their cabins on the other side of the athletic field.

Andy gave me a puzzled look.

"Believe me now?" I asked.

He didn't answer.

"Want some advice?" I asked.

Josh and Andy nodded.

"Save your snacks. You're gonna hate lunch."

32

I started toward my cabin. Up ahead I saw
Peter's white shopping bag split and all his
stuff spill out onto the ground. The cool guys
were right behind him. My first inclination was to
hurry up and help him. But on second thought I
decided not to. Before I could help Peter, I had to
concentrate on figuring out how to help myself
get out of the mess I was in.

Just as on the previous days, the cool guys
started to hassle Peter about his Water Pik. I
went around them and continued lugging my duffle bag toward the cabin. But it wasn't long before
the cool guys, with their lighter bags, passed me.

This time I got to the cabin about the same
time as Lewis. Inside, the cool guys had already
staked out the back two bunks. Lewis and I put
down our duffle bags and glanced at each other. I
pointed at the bunk closest to the front of the
cabin.

"Want to share this one?" I asked.

Lewis nodded.

"Top or bottom?" I asked.

"I'll take the top," he said.

"You don't want to take that one, Sleeping Beauty," Zack said from his bunk in the back of the cabin. "Only the dweebs want to be close to the counselor."

"Come on back here with us," said Rick. "You can take the top of my bunk."

"No, thanks," I said, and started to unpack.

Peter was the last camper to enter the cabin. The only bed left was the top of Rick's double decker. Peter lugged his stuff toward it.

Zack turned to Rick. "Must be your lucky day," he said with a snigger.

Lewis and I glanced at each other, but said nothing.

Once again it took a while to get all my stuff unpacked. I knew I had to do something different if I wanted to get out of the first day of camp, but I still didn't know what to do. Then Marty arrived and showed us how the cabin worked. After he left for the waterfront, Zack strolled toward my bunk. Lewis was on top, tacking up his car pictures. Zack went through the small, fast car routine. Lewis told him to get lost, thereby earning the nickname of Mighty Mouse.

"So we got Mighty Mouse and Sleeping Beauty in the first bunk," Zack said, taunting us.

Lewis stuck another picture on the rafter and didn't say a word.

Zack turned to me. "Wanna play some tetherball, Sleeping Beauty?"

"No, thanks," I replied.

"What's wrong?" Zack said. "You chicken, Sleeping Beauty? Maybe we'll have to call you Sleeping Chicken."

"Or Chicken Beauty," added Dan.

"The mucous brain says, 'What?' " I said.

"What?" said Zack.

I caught Rick's eye. He smiled.

Zack put his hands on his hips. "Man, what a winner cabin we've got this year. Mighty Mouse, Sleeping Chicken, and Gummi Bear."

Following Lewis's lead, I ignored him. Zack turned to Peter and challenged him to play tetherball. When Peter admitted he didn't know what tetherball was, Zack and Dan made fun of him.

A few moments later, Peter, Dan, and Zack went outside to play. This time Rick followed, then stopped by the screen door until the others had gone outside. I was surprised to see him turn to Lewis and me.

"You guys coming?" he asked.

Lewis and I both shook our heads. Rick paused for a moment as if he wasn't certain what to do. Then he went outside.

As soon as Rick had gone, Lewis went to the

screen door and looked out. We could hear Zack and Dan laughing as Zack humiliated Peter in tetherball. Inside, Lewis just watched.

Meanwhile, I kept wondering how I was ever going to get out of the first day of camp.

33

Later we all went to the dining hall for lunch. I walked alone, a dozen yards behind Zack, Rick, and Dan. Behind me Lewis and Peter talked quietly.

Just as on the first day, I wondered what they were talking about. This time I slowed my pace and tried to eavesdrop.

"You have to stand up to them," Lewis was saying. "If you don't, they're going to make you miserable the whole time you're here."

I slowed up even more. Now I was walking with them. Peter gave me a nervous look out of the corner of his eye.

"There's one thing I don't get," I said quietly to Lewis. "When you stood up to Zack before, how'd you know he wouldn't just haul back and smash you?"

"I didn't know for sure," Lewis said. "But I figured he'd have to be really stupid to do something

114

like that on the first day of camp. Besides, I think he's mostly talk."

Peter just listened, but didn't say anything.

Once again, Josh, Andy, and I met before lunch.

"Still think you're trapped in the first day of camp?" Josh asked.

"I don't *think* it," I said. "I *know* it."

Josh and Andy shared an uncomfortable look.

"So how's it going with the cool guys and Peter the dweeb?" Andy asked.

"They're really giving him grief," I said.

"You standing up for him?" Andy asked.

"That doesn't work," I said.

Andy and Josh gave each other another funny look.

"What do you mean?" asked Andy.

"I mean I tried it yesterday and it didn't work," I said.

"You tried what yesterday?" Josh asked.

"I protected Peter from the cool guys," I said.

"Jake, I'm really getting worried about you," Andy said. "We keep telling you that you weren't here yesterday."

"And I keep telling you I was," I said. "You think I want to spend the rest of my life trapped in the first day of camp, eating American Chop Suey for lunch every day?"

Josh wrinkled his nose. "What's American Chop Suey?"

"You'll know in about a minute," I said.

Both Josh and Andy were quiet for a moment. Then Josh said, "Okay, Jake, for the sake of argument, let's say you really are stuck in the first day of camp. What are Andy and I supposed to do about it?"

That was a good question.

"I don't know," I said. "But it definitely feels better knowing that someone believes me."

By now, Mr. Maller was standing at the microphone. He began his speech welcoming us to camp.

"Guess we better get back to our tables," Josh said.

"See you later, Jake." Andy said.

"One last thing," I said. "Whatever you do this afternoon, *don't* go on the nature walk."

Josh and Andy gave me bewildered looks. Then shaking their heads in puzzlement, they went back to their tables.

34

By the time I got back to my table, Peter was twisted around in his seat, listening to Mr. Maller's welcoming speech. Dan was reaching across the table and putting the plastic wrap over Peter's glass.

I locked eyes with Lewis, and we shared a knowing look. But then he looked away. I just didn't get it. If protecting Peter wasn't the right thing to do, then what was? Certainly not joining the cool guys and picking on him. What other choice was there?

Mr. Maller's speech ended. The camp waiters were coming out of the kitchen with big trays of American Chop Suey. Meanwhile, Zack reached for the metal pitcher in the middle of the table. "Who wants bug juice?"

"Me, me, me, me." Everyone at the table said they wanted some.

"Here you go." Zack stood up and poured out the bug juice. Just as he had on the first day, he held the pitcher high so that a long red stream cascaded into the glass in front of each kid.

Finally every glass except Peter's was filled.

"So, Gummi Bear, you sure you want some?" Zack asked.

Peter nodded.

I just couldn't stand the idea of him getting splattered with bug juice again. Maybe stopping Zack wasn't the right thing to do, but I had to do it anyway.

"Hey, Peter," I said. "Look at your glass."

Peter looked down at his glass. His eyes widened.

"Bombs away." Zack poured.

Peter pulled his glass away and slid his chair back to avoid getting splattered.

Splash! The red bug juice hit the table and splattered in every direction. A little of it landed on Peter, but this time more hit Marty.

"Hey!" Marty jumped up, glowering at Zack. "What'd you do that for?"

"It's not my fault Gummi Bear pulled his glass away," Zack said.

"Yeah, but look." Peter shoved the plastic-covered glass to Marty, who'd grabbed a handful of napkins and started to blot the bug juice off his shirt.

"Who put the plastic on Peter's glass?" Marty asked, looking at Zack and Dan. Neither of them answered. Marty nodded knowingly just the same.

Zack put down the pitcher and sat down looking pretty ticked.

"The bonehead says, 'What?' " I mumbled.

"What?" said Zack.

I winked at Lewis, but he just looked back at me with a blank expression.

The only person who smiled was Rick.

35

After lunch the cool guys went off to play basketball. Peter asked me if I wanted to go on the nature walk with him. I said I appreciated his asking, but I wasn't up to it.

This time I went down to the waterfront. When I got there, Lewis was standing on a dock lined with small blue sailboats. He was talking to an older guy wearing a gray counselor's T-shirt. When Lewis saw me, he waved. "Hey, Jake, got a second?"

I went over. "What's up?"

"I was thinking about taking a boat out, but they have a rule that you have to sail with a buddy," Lewis said. "Want to go?"

"I don't know how to sail," I said.

"No sweat," said Lewis. "I'll do everything."

A few minutes later I was sitting in the bow of a sailboat. Lewis was in the stern, steering with the rudder and pulling the ropes attached to the white sail overhead.

The breeze on the lake moved us along at an even pace. Not exactly thrilling, but it was relaxing.

"Thanks for coming," Lewis said.

"No prob," I said. "So you like sailing, huh?"

"Naw, I hate it." Lewis smiled a little to let me know he was kidding.

I reached over the side and dipped my hand in the lake. "Brrr, the water's cold."

"Better get used to it," Lewis said.

"Why?"

"Because first thing every morning Marty's gonna make us swim."

"First thing in the morning!?" I gasped. "Are you serious?"

Lewis nodded. "Marty's a swim instructor. I know a guy who was in his cabin last year. He said Marty always makes his cabin do it."

"Bummer," I said.

Lewis agreed. Then we talked about where Lewis learned to sail, and about the sailboat his parents shared with another family. It was sort of strange — how friendly and talkative he was on the sailboat when he was so quiet everywhere else.

"As long as I get to sail, this is gonna be a good summer," he said.

"Too bad it won't be good for Peter," I said. "Not with those dipwads picking on him all the time."

"I told him he has to stand up to them," Lewis said.

"Yeah, I know," I said. "But I'm starting to think maybe he doesn't know how."

"Maybe it doesn't matter," Lewis said with a shrug. "Maybe Zack and his friends will get bored picking on Peter and find other things to do."

From the previous days I knew that wouldn't happen. "Er, I doubt it. I think they're planning to mess him up pretty good tonight."

Lewis nodded, but didn't answer.

We sailed around the lake for a while more. There wasn't much for me to do, so I just thought about stuff.

And that's when I had the idea for helping Peter.

It was risky, but it just might work.

36

Once again, everybody met at the cabin before dinner. Even though I hadn't played basketball that afternoon, I still decided to take a shower. When I came out of the bathroom, Zack was bugging Peter about the nature walk again.

"What are you, some kind of freak?" Zack asked.

Peter bowed his head.

"Hey, Zack . . ." Rick started to say.

"Yeah, what?" Zack snapped.

"Maybe you should leave the guy alone," Rick said.

"Guy?" Zack smirked and stared straight at Peter. "I don't see a guy. I don't know what I see. It's like something from another planet."

Rick didn't answer. He just looked at me.

"The fleabrain says, 'What?' " I muttered.

"What?" said Zack.

Rick grinned.

"Shower's free," I said.

Zack went into the bathroom. Rick and I both watched him. Then we turned and looked at each other. Whose side was he really on? I wondered.

"What happened to you guys?" I asked Josh and Andy outside the dining hall before dinner that night. They were both covered with red welts.

"We went on the nature walk," Andy said, scratching a bunch of swollen lumps on his neck.

"Are you serious?" I gasped. "That's exactly what I told you *not* to do."

"Yeah, but we had to find out why you didn't want us to do it," Josh said, scratching his arm.

"Because you'd get eaten alive by mosquitos," I said.

"We found that out," said Andy as he scratched his ear.

"So, you still think you're trapped in the first day of camp?" Josh asked.

"I don't *think* it," I said. "I *know* it."

Josh and Andy gave each other a skeptical look. Then Josh said, "Okay, listen, we had a talk. We still find this really hard to believe, Jake. But then, we never would have believed that you could get stuck in the President's body, or that Andy would switch bodies with your dog. So just in case it's true, is there anything we can do to help?"

"You guys still have your Cheese Whiz?" I asked.

After dinner we went back to the cabin. Zack and Dan talked in low voices as they planned what they were going to do to Peter later. Then Dan went into the bathroom and stayed forever. After a while, Marty got impatient and called into the bathroom to ask Dan if he was okay, and Dan called back that he'd be out in a second. Then Zack made the joke about being lost and everyone laughed.

Meanwhile, I turned to Lewis and Peter. "Why don't we wait outside?" I suggested.

As soon as Peter and Lewis came outside, I told them what the cool guys were planning to do to Peter.

"They can't sneak out during the movie," Peter said. "Marty won't let them."

"Marty won't be there to stop them," I said.

Lewis frowned. "How do you know?"

"Uh . . ." I couldn't tell him the truth. "I heard some other counselors talking. They said they were going to get together during the movie and try to figure out how to meet the counselors from the girls' camp. I have to believe Marty will be interested."

Lewis gave me a sly grin. "Yeah, well, you're probably right about that."

"If you know what Zack's planning," Peter said, "why don't you tell Marty. Then he'll talk to them."

"Talking to them won't change anything," I said.

Peter gave Lewis a questioning look.

"He's probably right," Lewis said.

Then I told them my plan. Well, not *all* of it. But most of it.

"I don't know, Jake." Peter swallowed nervously when I'd finished. "If it doesn't work, they could make us really miserable for the next month."

"I'm willing to take that risk," I said. "And if you don't try it, your life is gonna be miserable for the next month anyway. Why not give it a shot? At least this way there's a *chance* things could turn out okay."

Peter's shoulders sagged and he stared at the ground. "Maybe I should just go home. I didn't want to come to camp in the first place."

"You can't just quit," I said. "You can't run away your whole life. Just because you like different things than they do doesn't mean they're better than you and you're worse. You're just different, Peter. And you have to stand up and face them."

Peter bit his lip and glanced at Lewis, who nodded back as if he agreed with me.

Peter let out a big sigh. "Okay. Let's try it."

37

Later I sat on the bench in the back of the dining hall with Peter and Lewis. At my feet was Andy's one-million candle power SuperBeam flashlight, which I'd asked him to lend me along with the Cheese Whiz. As soon as the movie started, Marty warned us not to get into any trouble, and left. Then the cool guys disappeared.

"Ready?" I whispered to Peter and Lewis.

"I don't know," Peter whispered back nervously. "You sure this is a good idea?"

"No," I whispered. "But can you think of anything better?"

Peter shook his head.

"Then let's do it," I said.

The crickets were chirping in the moonlight. Lewis, Peter, and I snuck around the back of the cabins until we got to B-13. Inside the cabin we could hear whispers and the squeak of bedsprings as the cool guys set their booby traps.

Lewis and I opened our day packs, which we'd hidden behind the cabin before going to the dining hall to see the movie. We took out rope and the cans of Cheese Whiz. Then Lewis and Peter got out their flashlights. I was already carrying Andy's SuperBeam.

"Ready?" I whispered.

"Ready," Lewis replied.

We quietly snuck around to the front of the cabin. Inside the cool guys were still setting up their booby traps. But when the front door creaked, they looked up.

Click! Click! Click!

Lewis, Peter, and I flicked on our flashlights and aimed the beams right into their eyes. Lewis got Dan, Peter got Rick, and I got Zack with the SuperBeam. They all cowered, holding up their hands to block the bright light, squinting as they tried to see.

"Hey! What's going on?"

"Turn those things off!"

"Stop shining it in my eyes!"

We kept the flashlights on, blinding them, and didn't say a word.

"Who are you guys?" Dan asked.

I nudged Peter.

"Uh, we are the Dork Protection Posse," Peter said.

"What?"

"The Dork Protection Posse," Peter repeated.

"We protect dorks against those who seek to do them harm."

"Wait a minute." Zack straightened up. Even though the SuperBeam was still blinding him, he smiled. "I know who you are. You're Gummi Bear. And I bet your buddies are Sleeping Beauty and Mighty Mouse."

"The Dork Protection Posse, huh?" Dan said with a nasty grin.

Still shielding his eyes from the lights, Zack took a step toward us. "Isn't that cute?" he asked. "The Dork Protection Posse has come to protect the dork."

"Yeah," added Dan. "But who's gonna protect the Dork Protection Posse?"

They came toward us. Peter took a step back and glanced at me. "Now what?"

38

Zack and Dan were closing in on us. Peter, Lewis, and I backed toward the wall.

"I thought we were gonna get back up help," Peter said nervously.

"I thought so too," I said.

"So where is it?" Peter asked.

"Good question," I answered, glancing at Rick.

Dan and Zack were getting closer. We kept our flashlights on their faces, but it didn't stop them.

"This was a really great idea, Jake," Lewis muttered sarcastically.

"Hey, I only said we should try it, okay?" I shot back. "I never promised you it would work."

Meanwhile, Zack was rolling up the sleeves of his shirt. "I think the Dork Protection Posse is about to become the *Dead* Protection Posse."

"Yeah," said Dan. "Dead Meat."

They were only a few feet away now. I looked at Rick again. This time I caught his eye.

"Wait a minute, guys," Rick said.

Zack and Dan stopped. "What is it?" Zack asked.

"This is dumb," Rick said. "Somehow they found out we were playing a trick on them, so they decided to play a trick on us. I don't see why it has to turn into an all-out rumble."

"You chicken?" Zack sneered.

"No, I'm not chicken," Rick shot back. "I just don't see the point in hurting them. They didn't do anything to us."

"That's right," Zack said. "And now I'm gonna make *sure* they don't do anything to us."

It was time to make my move. I quickly muttered, "The bozo says, 'What?' "

"What?" Zack frowned.

Rick grinned.

"Come on, Rick," I said. "You know what I'm talking about."

The smile disappeared from Rick's face.

Zack stopped and looked back at Rick. "What's he talking about?"

"Peabrain says, 'What?' " I said.

"*What?*" Zack spun around and wrinkled his forehead.

Rick grinned again.

"It'll be four against two," I said to Rick.

"Huh?" Zack looked back and forth between us. "What's going on?"

Rick looked uncertain.

"Now I get it," Lewis whispered. "He's the back up?"

I nodded and looked at Rick. "Come on, man. This way they'll leave Peter alone and we'll all have a decent month."

"What?" said Zack.

"That's what the veghead said," I said.

Rick grinned.

"Veghead?" Zack scowled.

"Hey, I get it!" Dan gasped. "The veghead says, 'What?'"

Zack turned. "What?"

"That's what the veghead said," Dan tried to explain.

Meanwhile, the rest of us rolled our eyes and grinned.

"The . . . veghead . . . says . . . 'What?'" Zack muttered to himself. Suddenly his eyes widened. "The bozo says, 'What?' . . . The bonehead says, 'What?' . . . The peabrain says 'What?'"

He finally understood.

Zack grit his teeth, balled his hands into fists, and spun to face me. There was murder in his eyes. "Why you . . ."

I quickly looked at Rick. Now I *really* needed him. But Rick just gave me a stony stare.

39

Zack came toward me, prepared to kill. I dropped the SuperBeam and raised my fists. Next to me, Peter and Lewis did the same thing.

The only way we were going down was swinging. But against Dan and Zack we wouldn't have a chance.

"Hold it," Rick said.

Zack stopped. "Why?"

Rick walked around him and stood with Lewis, Peter, and me. "If you take on Jake, you take us all on."

Zack narrowed his eyes. "What's with you?"

"I'm just tired of you picking on people," Rick said. "You never pick on anyone who'll fight back. I think that makes you the biggest chicken of all."

Zack sputtered and snarled, he cursed at us and said a lot of nasty stuff. But Rick was right. When it was four against two, Zack didn't want to fight.

40

L ater that night I stood by my bunk, speaking quietly to Rick and Lewis.

"Thanks, guys," I said. "It wouldn't have worked without you."

"I'm glad you got me to do it," Lewis said. "Otherwise, I probably would have just stuck to myself, thinking I was lucky they were picking on Peter and not me."

Rick nodded. "I know what you mean."

"Get in your bunks, guys," Marty said.

I got into bed feeling confident that I'd done the right thing. Although I was sort of disappointed that we didn't get to dangle Zack and Dan from the rafters and give them Super Cheese Whiz Wedgies.

I hadn't picked on Peter, and I hadn't protected him either. I'd helped him learn how to protect himself. That *had* to be the right thing to do. And hopefully it would be my ticket into the second day of camp, and to an okay time for the rest of the month.

Despite the lumpy pillow and itchy blanket, I slept soundly that night.

der or chased us till they dind time flute seems
the pond.

Escape the bump guide, and keep his even!
left soundly. But this is

41

DAY FOUR

I felt a bump and opened my eyes. *Huh!?* What was I doing on the bus again?

We were pulling into the parking lot.

No! NO! *NO!*

Not again!

It couldn't be!

It wasn't fair!

"You can't do this to me!" I shouted angrily. "I did everything right! I did everything I possibly could! I've been *good!*"

Every head on the bus turned.

"You don't get it," I told them. "I've been here before. I've done this."

They all stared at me. A sea of frowns. They thought I was crazy.

I turned to Zack, Dan, and Rick in the back of the bus. "Zack, you're gonna pick on Peter today. You're gonna challenge him to one-handed, one-

136

footed tetherball. You're gonna put plastic wrap on his glass so that the bug juice spills on him, and put detergent in his Water Pik. Dan, you're gonna go along with whatever Zack does because you're just a follower. Rick, you're gonna go along with Zack, too, even though you don't like it. Deep down inside you don't like picking on people, but you feel like you're stuck with Zack because it's important for you to be cool."

I turned to Lewis. "You're gonna stay out of it, Lewis. Zack's going to pick on you a little, but you're going to stand up to him."

"How do you know I have a Water Pik?" Peter asked from his seat.

"Believe me, I know," I said.

"What about Andy and me?" Josh asked.

"You guys aren't involved in this," I said. "Your cabins are on the other side of the athletic field. But hold onto your Cheeze Whiz and crackers. You're gonna need that stuff after you see what they serve for lunch."

Zack, Dan, and Rick gave me strange looks as they passed my seat and got off the bus.

Peter, Andy, and Josh were still looking at me like I'd lost my marbles.

Why was I still in the first day of camp?

What could I possibly have done wrong?

Lewis stood up and got off the bus, followed by Peter.

Now only Josh, Andy, and I were left on the

bus. They stood up and slung their day packs over their shoulders.

"Aren't you getting off?" Andy asked.

And go through all that garbage again? I shook my head.

"You have to get off the bus, Jake," Josh said.

"No way," I said. "I'm not doing this again."

"You're not doing *what* again?" Andy asked.

There was no point in explaining. They wouldn't believe me, and it made no difference anyway.

But if I didn't get off the bus, then I wouldn't have to go through the first day of camp again.

"Uh, boys?" Down at the front of the bus Mr. Maller had climbed back on. "Time to get off and get your bags."

I stayed seated. Andy and Josh gave me worried looks.

"Come on," Andy whispered urgently. "They want you off the bus."

I crossed my arms and shook my head. "No way."

"Come on, boys," Mr. Maller said. "We need this bus."

"Jake, for the last time," Josh pleaded.

"Go on," I said. "Have a great camp experience."

Josh and Andy frowned at each other, then looked back at me.

"Are you serious?" Josh asked. "We wouldn't even be here if it weren't for you."

"Yeah, this whole thing was your idea," Andy said.

"I'm sure you'll have a great time," I said.

"Boys?" Mr. Maller said. "Is something wrong?"

Josh turned to him. "Yeah, our friend Jake won't get off the bus."

The corners of Mr. Maller's mouth fell. I doubt he needed this kind of aggravation on the first day of camp. He came down the aisle toward me.

"What's your name, son?" he asked.

I told him.

"We need this bus back," he said. "You have to get off."

"Listen, Mr. Maller," I said. "I'm really sorry to do this to you, but there's no way I'm getting off this bus."

42

Mr. Maller talked to me for a long time. Then he got Marty to come talk to me.

Then they called the state police and got a trooper to come talk to me.

Then they called my parents and said they had to come get me.

Four hours later my dad got there. I was still sitting in the bus. Dad wasn't happy.

I put my duffle bag in our van and he drove me home.

"Why, Jake?" he asked on the way.

"I can't explain it, Dad," I said. "Just believe me. It has to be this way."

Dad shook his head and sighed. "Well, at least it was the first day. I can still get a refund."

We rode along in silence for a while. Then I remembered something.

"Hey, Dad, does Jessica know I'm coming home?"

"I don't see how she could," Dad replied. "She's over at the town pool, at work."

Good, I thought.

Later that afternoon I stood by the living room window and watched my sister come up the walk. Just as she reached the front door, I pulled it open.

"Ahhh!" she screeched. "Jake, what are you doing here?"

"I want my donuts," I growled.

"*What!?*" She stared at me in wide-eyed disbelief.

"You heard me. I want my donuts."

Her jaw dropped. "You . . . you came all the way home from camp to get your donuts?"

"Nobody takes my donuts."

"Are you crazy?"

"*Just give me my donuts!*"

"I . . . I can't," she stammered. "I ate them."

"Then I'm gonna *cut* them out of you." I went into the kitchen and came back with a dull butter knife.

When I got back to the front door, it was wide open. Jessica was running down the street as fast as she could.

That night I laid my head down on my nice soft feather pillow and pulled up my comfortable blanket. I couldn't remember being so glad to see my own bed.

After all, how can you be stuck in the first day of camp if you're not there?

43

DAY FIVE

I felt a bump and opened my eyes.

Oh, no! I was on the bus again.

This had to be some kind of joke.

A really bad, sick joke.

"Have a nice nap, Sleeping Beauty?" Zack asked.

Was there *nothing* I could do to get out of the first day of camp?

"What's the matter?" Zack asked. "Can't talk?"

But there *had* to be a way out. Last time it happened, when I was trapped in the first day of school, I'd figured out how to escape it.

That meant I was *still* doing something wrong.

I just had to figure out what it was.

"Hey, I'm talking to you," Zack said.

I had to think. I had to concentrate. I had to retrace my steps through the past four days. Somewhere in those days was the key, the missing link that would get me out of this mess.

"Hey," Zack said.

I looked up at him. "Bug off, wombat."

"Huh?" Zack started to make a fist.

"Lay off him," Rick said.

Zack glowered at me, but continued down the aisle and got off the bus.

Was I supposed to do something different with Peter? It didn't make sense. Somehow, deep inside, I knew that helping Peter learn to defend himself *was* the right thing to do.

But then why was I still trapped in the first day of camp? Was there *someone else* I had to help?

"Aren't you getting off?" Andy asked. He and Josh were standing with their day packs slung over their shoulders.

Did I really have to get off and go through it all again?

I guess I had to . . . until I figured out what to do.

That day I tried to do *everything* right.

I helped Peter learn to defend himself again.

I warned him about the plastic wrap.

I sailed with Lewis and got him to join the Dork Protection Posse.

I got Rick to take our side against Zack and Dan.

Finally, it was time to go to sleep.

I went into the bathroom and washed up.

I was halfway back to my bunk when I realized I'd forgotten to do something. It was something I'd forgotten to do *every* night since I'd gotten to camp.

But it couldn't be the answer, could it?

I wasn't going to take any chances.

I went back into the bathroom . . . and brushed my teeth.

44

DAY SIX

I felt a bump and opened my eyes.

I was on the bus again.

I was going through the first day of camp again!

I was going to look at American Chop Suey again!

"No! *No!*" I screamed.

I couldn't take it!

Everyone stared at me. I didn't care. I jumped out of my seat and ran to the front of the bus.

"Hey!" the driver shouted as I grabbed the wheel and jammed my foot against the gas pedal, flooring it.

Varrroooom! The bus's wheels spun wildly, spraying gravel around the parking lot. The bus lurched forward. Outside campers and counselors dove out of the way.

"Hey! What's he doing?" "Stop!" "Look out!" Inside the bus kids screamed as we hurtled over a log barrier and caromed across the grass toward the lake.

"*You're gonna kill us all!*" the bus driver shouted as we grappled over the steering wheel.

"*I don't care!*" I screamed. "*I — *"

"Hey, Jake, wake up!" Someone was shaking my shoulder. "Jake?"

I opened my eyes.

I was lying in my camp bunk. Marty, Peter, and Lewis were staring down at me. Marty's hand was on my shoulder.

"You okay?" he asked.

The sun was shining outside. The air had a fresh chilly morning smell. Despite my lumpy pillow and itchy blanket, I felt warm and cozy.

"Where am I?" I asked.

"Camp Walton," Marty said.

"What day is it?" I asked.

"The second day of camp," said Lewis.

"You must've had a bad dream," added Peter.

I sat up and rubbed my eyes.

"You okay now?" Marty asked.

"Uh . . . yeah . . . I guess." I nodded.

Was it possible?

Had I really gotten out of the first day of camp!?

Marty clapped his hands together. "Okay, guys, get your swimsuits on."

"What're you talking about?" Zack asked. "We haven't had breakfast yet."

"In this cabin we always take a nice cold swim in the lake before breakfast," Marty announced. "Come on, guys, let's go."

Everyone groaned.

I pulled my blanket up to my chin, dreading the thought of swimming in that freezing cold lake. If only I could be trapped in the first day of camp again!

HELP!

I'M TRAPPED IN MY
CAMP COUNSELOR'S BODY

To Emily, Adam, and Lucy Wickersham

NOTE

Hi, it's me, Jake Sherman, the kid who's always switching bodies with other people. I know that my stories sometimes get sort of funny, but before you read this book, I need to talk to you about something serious.

Everybody makes mistakes. No one likes to admit it, but we all goof up now and then. The truth is, even good, smart people sometimes make bad, dumb mistakes. They don't mean to, but, hey, it happens.

I just think that maybe we're a little too hard on people who make mistakes. Maybe we ought to lighten up when someone we know blows it big time.

Because next time it might be our turn to mess up. And we don't want people coming down hard on us for an honest mistake, do we?

Believe me, I know what I'm talking about.

PART ONE
THE ULTIMATE MESS-UP

1

"**A**t least it's not lamb brain tacos," said my friend Josh Hopka. "They're considered a delicacy in Mexico. Or sun-dried maggots. They love 'em in China."

It was the day before summer vacation, and my friends and I were eating lunch in the cafeteria. On the last day at Burt Ipchupt Middle School, they always served us something called Last Day Surprise.

This year it was a stew with greenish pieces of celery, chunks of potato, thin white strips of chicken, and orange disks of carrot, all floating in a light-colored sauce.

"Maybe it's chicken pot pie without the pie," I guessed, staring down at my plate.

"Or chicken chow mein without the rice," said my friend Andy Kent.

"For all we know, it could be yesterday's garbage without the flies," Josh added cheerfully.

"But at least it's not coconut-cream-marinated dog."

Josh had gotten a book of gross-outs from the school book fair and now at lunch he insisted on reading these disgusting recipes. He flipped to another page. "Maybe it's white ant pie, a very popular meal in Tanzania."

"Chill, Josh," I said. "You're starting to gross us out."

"Sure, Jake," Josh taunted me. "You'd want something easier to digest. Like broiled beetle grubs from Japan or maybe cooked baked bat from Samoa."

"That's a redundancy," Andy pointed out.

"A what?" I asked.

"It means Josh said something twice that he only had to say once," Andy explained. "He said baked so he didn't have to say cooked."

Josh made a face. "What's with you?"

"It's that English final we had this morning," Andy explained. "I can't get that stuff out of my head. Anyway, guys, just think, we're halfway through our last day of school."

Outside the trees were covered with new green leaves and kids were walking around in T-shirts and shorts.

"Yeah," said Josh as he speared a carrot with his fork and raised it toward his mouth. "And as bad as this lunch is, it probably beats what we'll be eating at that new camp Jake picked."

"No way," I protested. "Didn't you guys watch the video the camp sent?"

Josh and Andy shook their heads.

"My parents were too busy," Josh said. "They said if the camp was good enough for your parents, it had to be okay."

"And we got so many videos, after a while we gave up watching them," Andy said. "My dad says all camp videos are the same. They all show lakes and waterfronts."

"And ball fields and basketball courts," added Josh.

"And camp-outs with kids roasting marshmallows and singing dumb camp songs," said Andy.

"Seen one, seen 'em all," Josh concluded.

"Not the camp I picked for us *this* year," I said proudly.

2

I was just about to tell my friends about our new camp when Mr. Dirksen came by.

"Jake, could you come to the science lab with me?" he asked. "Something urgent has come up and I must speak with you."

Mr. Dirksen was our science teacher and the inventor of the Dirksen Intelligence Transfer System, or DITS.

"Uh, sure." I got up and looked at my friends. "Catch you later, guys."

Mr. Dirksen and I left the cafeteria and started down the hall to the science lab.

"What are your plans for the summer, Jake?" he asked.

"My friends and I are going to camp again," I answered as we pushed open the door to the science lab.

Inside was the DITS. It was a fairly large invention consisting of a computer terminal and two lounge chairs. Mr. Dirksen had originally invented it with the idea of transferring knowledge from one person to another. But all it really did was make people switch bodies.

"Are you going to leave the DITS here in school for the summer?" I asked.

"That one, yes," answered Mr. Dirksen as he closed the lab door behind him.

"That one?" I scowled. "I thought there was only one DITS."

Mr. Dirksen gave me a jaunty smile. "Can you keep a secret, Jake?"

"Sure."

"I assumed you could," Mr. Dirksen said. "After all, I know that you've switched bodies with your dog, the President of the United States, an alien, and no doubt others you haven't told me about. And yet you've managed not to tell many people."

"It's not like anyone would believe me," I replied.

"Well, I'm going to tell you about something people just might believe," my teacher said. "And that's why I need your promise that you won't tell a soul."

He pulled open a desk drawer and took out a small tape player with two sets of headphones attached to it. "Do you know what this is, Jake?"

"It's a Walkman," I answered.

"No." Mr. Dirksen shook his head. "This . . . is the mini-DITS. It's the same as the original machine, but I've made it much smaller."

"Cool!" I said. "Does it transfer intelligence or just switch bodies?"

Mr. Dirksen let out a defeated sigh. "It only switches bodies, I'm afraid. I've given up on trying to transfer intelligence."

"No offense or anything," I said, "but it's about time."

Mr. Dirksen handed the mini-DITS to me. "I want you to keep this for the summer, Jake."

"Why?" I asked.

"Kim and I have been invited on a rafting expedition up the Amazon River. It's going to be fantastically interesting but also very dangerous."

Kim was Ms. Rogers, my social studies teacher. She was married to Mr. Dirksen, but she still went by her old name.

"I'm worried that if anything happens to me," said Mr. Dirksen, "the world will never learn about my invention."

"You *want* the world to know about the DITS?" I asked, surprised.

"Oh, yes, absolutely," Mr. Dirksen said. "But not until I've tested this new model. So I want you to take it for the summer. After all," he chuckled, "you should be able to survive camp without much difficulty."

He put his hand on my shoulder and gave me a serious look. "If anything should happen to me, Jake, I want you to carry on my work."

"You mean you want me to be a middle school science teacher?" I asked.

"No, no, not *that* work," Mr. Dirksen said, then pointed at the mini-DITS. "*This* work."

"Uh, okay, sure." I tucked the mini-DITS under my arm. "I promise I'll take good care of it."

"Just remember that the mini-DITS has never been tested," Mr. Dirksen reminded me. "So no fooling around with it."

"You got it, Mr. D," I said.

Mr. Dirksen patted me on the shoulder and walked me toward the door. "So, Jake, are you and your friends going back to last summer's camp?"

"Nope," I said. "I picked a new one this year."

"What's its name?" asked my teacher.

"Camp Gromly or Gramly or something," I said.

Mr. Dirksen raised his eyebrows curiously. "You're not sure of the name?"

"Not exactly," I admitted. "I went through so many camps that I get mixed up. But don't worry, I've got the name written down at home."

3

"What was the Dorkman's urgent news?" Josh asked later as he, Andy, and I walked home from school.

"Uh, nothing," I said.

Josh made a face. "What is this, a secret?"

"So isn't this cool, guys?" I said. "School's over! It's summer!"

"Know what, Jake?" Andy smirked. "That was the lamest attempt at changing the subject I've ever seen."

"Fess up, Jake," Josh insisted.

"Look, it was nothing," I said. "The Dorkman and Ms. Rogers are going on a dangerous expedition to the Amazon, and he just wanted me to promise that if anything happened to him, I'd carry on with his work."

Andy made a face. "You mean, be a middle school science teacher?"

"No, his work on the DITS." I stopped and showed them the mini-DITS.

"Way cool!" Andy gasped. "Does it do the same thing as the DITS?"

"Dirksen *thinks* so, but he isn't sure," I said. "He hasn't tested it yet. He just wants me to keep it safe for the summer."

"You going to leave it at home?" asked Josh.

I shook my head. "And let my sister Jessica find it in my closet? No way. I guess I'll have to take it to camp with me."

"So tell us about this great new camp," Andy said.

I grinned. "It's the only one with its own video arcade."

Josh and Andy stared at me. "You serious?"

I nodded. "And bunks with cable TV and VCRs. And a heated swimming pool. And instead of camp food, every meal is catered by McDonald's."

Josh and Andy both went slack-jawed. *"No way!"*

"Better believe it," I said.

Andy and Josh grinned and raised their palms. We all shared a high five. "Way to go, Jake!"

"There's just one thing, guys," I cautioned them. "If our parents find out what this camp is really like, they could still change their minds at the last minute."

"Good point," agreed Josh. "My parents always talk about how wonderful it is to rough it in the great outdoors. If they find out about the cable TV and fast food, they'll wig."

"So don't say nothing about it," I told them.

"That's a double negative," Andy corrected me. "You should have said, don't say *anything*."

I frowned. "Maybe you're right, but school's over. Forget about English."

"Yeah," agreed Josh. "It's time to start planning our summer of leisure."

4

A week later, early on a Sunday morning, Andy's parents drove us to the Jeffersonville mall. The bus to Camp Grimley would pick us up in the parking lot.

"You think they'll have Night Mission?" Josh whispered to Andy and me in the back of the car.

"What's that?" Andy whispered back.

"This totally cool new video game," Josh explained in a low voice. "You're the head of this platoon sent into the jungle on a night mission. You get to use night-vision glasses and stuff. It's awesome."

Meanwhile, in the front seat, Andy's mom, Mrs. Kent, shifted uneasily. "I feel so guilty about this. We're sending Andy to a camp we know nothing about. I've been so busy I never got around to watching the camp video or calling anyone for references. All we know is that the Shermans and the Hopkas are sending Jake and Josh there."

"If it's good enough for them, it's good enough for us," said Mr. Kent.

"Besides," Andy said from the backseat, "I'll be with my two best friends. How bad could it be?"

"I guess you're right." His mom seemed to relax. "I just feel bad that we didn't do a better job for you."

"Don't worry, Mom," said Andy. Then he gave Josh and me a wink. "Everything's going to be fine."

When we got to the mall, the parking lot was filled with cars. Parents and campers were milling around everywhere.

"Gee," said Mr. Kent, "Grimley must be one popular camp."

"Don't be silly," Mrs. Kent said. "They're not all waiting for the Camp Grimley bus. Buses stop here to pick up campers for dozens of camps."

"How are we going to know where to wait?" Andy asked.

"Over there." Josh pointed to a sign that said "Camp Grimley." The sign was written by hand on a torn piece of cardboard and taped to a light pole. We walked over. No one else was there.

"I guess we're the only ones going from this area," Josh said.

We scoped out the crowd in the parking lot. Each camp had a spot for its campers to gather.

"How come other camps have big, fancy banners and flags while we just have a torn piece of cardboard?" Josh asked.

I motioned my friends to come close so Andy's parents wouldn't hear. "It just shows you how smart the owners are," I whispered. "Instead of wasting money on dumb things like banners, I bet they spent it on totally awesome game systems."

"Then they'll *definitely* have Night Mission," Josh said hopefully.

"Hey, look!" Andy pointed at the entrance to the parking lot where a big, shiny bus was pulling in. "Oh, cool, it's a deluxe motor coach! The kind with the little TVs! I bet that's ours!"

My friends and I watched eagerly as the bus wound its way through the parking lot . . . but then stopped at another camp sign.

Josh's shoulders sagged with disappointment. "Guess that isn't our bus."

"Don't worry," I said confidentially. "Ours will be just as cool."

More buses arrived to pick up campers, but none of them were from Camp Grimley. Even the familiar old green Camp Walton bus showed up. After a while, the parking lot started to empty out.

Mrs. Kent looked worried. "I hope they didn't forget us."

Josh and Andy shot me a concerned glance.

"Hey, it's no big deal," I said. "We're probably their last stop."

Bang! An explosion made us jump. A ramshackle old bus backfired as it trundled into the parking lot, trailing a long white plume of smoky exhaust.

"Oh, no!" Josh groaned.

Andy turned to me. "Don't tell me this is another one of Camp Grimley's money-saving ideas."

I didn't know what to say. The old bus creaked and squeaked as it rolled toward us. Suddenly it veered away and stopped next to a sign that said "Camp Run-a-Muck."

"Phew!" Josh sighed with relief. "I'm glad we don't go to *that* camp."

But the words were hardly out of his mouth when yet another vehicle swung into the parking lot. This one wasn't even a bus. It was an olive-green truck with a canvas tarp over the cargo area — like an Army troop carrier.

The truck stopped right in front of us. A guy with a blond crew cut jumped out. He was wearing a tight olive-green T-shirt and green camouflage pants.

"Going to Camp Grimley?" he asked.

My friends and I nodded, dumbfounded.

"What are you waiting for?" the guy said. "Climb on in. We're movin' out!"

The next thing we knew, he grabbed our backpacks and hurled them into the truck. Then he told us to step up on the back bumper and climb in under the tarp.

"Come on, pork chop, we don't have all day," the crew-cut guy barked when Josh hesitated.

166

Josh climbed in. Andy and I followed. We sat down on a wooden bench. Across from us sat a row of kids.

The crew-cut guy climbed in front and started the engine.

"Excuse me, sir," I heard Andy's mom say outside. "Are you really going to Camp Grimley?"

"Yes, ma'am," the crew-cut guy answered.

"Why aren't they going in a bus?" Mrs. Kent asked.

"I'll tell you why, ma'am," the crew-cut guy replied. "It's because buses are for wimps."

The truck lurched and pulled out of the mall parking lot.

Like it or not, we were on our way to Camp Grimley.

5

In the back of the truck, the two rows of ten campers faced each other with our backpacks piled on the floor between us. Five campers were girls. The rest were boys. We held on tight as the truck bounced and banged along.

Josh glared at me. "If this is another way Camp Grimley saves money for its video systems, they better have Night Mission *Deluxe*."

I didn't answer. This wasn't what I'd expected. I looked across the truck at the campers facing us. "Anybody know anything about Camp Grimley?"

"All I know is my parents picked it for me," said a chubby kid with brown hair parted in the middle.

"My dad said it would be a good experience," added a tall kid who seemed to be all knees and elbows.

"My uncle went there when he was young," said a girl with black lipstick, spiky black hair, and a pierced eyebrow. "He says it changed his life."

A guy sitting at the end of the bench shook his head and smirked at us. He was super-thin, with a buzz cut and a toothpick stuck behind his ear. He was wearing a black T-shirt with the sleeves cut off. On his right biceps was a tattoo of a snake.

"You look like you know something," I said to him.

"I know that by this time tomorrow you guys'll wish you never got on this truck," he replied.

"Why?" asked the tall kid who was all elbows and knees.

"Because Grimley is a survival camp," said the thin kid with the toothpick.

"What's that?" asked the girl with the spiky hair and black lipstick.

"A camp where the only thing you do is try to survive," the thin kid with the toothpick answered. "You have to find or kill your own food. You sleep on the ground and the only running water is what runs in the streams."

"Bull," I challenged him. "I saw the video they sent. How can it be a survival camp if they have cable TV, a heated pool, and the meals are catered by McDonald's?"

"Wait, I saw that video," said the chubby kid with the brown hair.

"See?" I said to the thin kid with the toothpick. "I'm not the only one."

"There's just one problem," said the chubby kid. "That wasn't a video from Camp Grimley."

6

A hush fell over the campers sitting in the back of the truck.

"What do you mean, it wasn't Camp Grimley?" Josh asked the chubby kid.

"It was another camp," the chubby kid answered. "I think it was called Camp Gramerly or something. Camp Grimley never sent a video."

"That's the most ridiculous thing I ever heard!" I sputtered. "You really think I'd be dumb enough to mix up the names of camps?"

Josh and Andy both nodded.

"Gee, thanks for having so much faith in me," I muttered sourly.

"I bet it *is* a survival camp," mumbled the tall kid who was all elbows and knees. "My father always says I'm too soft and I need to get tougher. He'd never send me to a camp with cable TV and a heated pool."

Josh leveled his gaze at me. "Way to go, Jake."

"Wait a minute!" I cried nervously and pointed at the girl with the spiky hair and black lipstick. "Didn't you say your uncle went to Camp Grimley?"

The spiky-haired girl nodded.

"And didn't he tell you it changed his life?" I asked.

"Yeah," said the girl.

"Did he tell you *how* it changed his life?" Josh asked her.

"Not really."

"He must've told you something," Andy said.

The spiky-haired girl shook her head. "That's all he ever says. Just, 'Camp Grimley changed my life,' over and over again. And then he gets this glassy look in his eyes and he starts to shake. And sometimes he even screams. And that's when the nurses come and take him back to the ward for his medication."

"The ward?" Josh repeated with a frown.

"Yeah," said the spiky-haired girl. "You know. The hospital ward."

"How long has he been in the hospital?" I asked.

"Ever since he came back."

"Came back from what?" asked Josh.

"Camp Grimley."

7

It wasn't long before we'd questioned every kid on the truck and learned the following:

1) No one had ever *seen* a video about Camp Grimley.

2) Except for the girl with the crazy uncle, no one *knew* anyone who had ever gone to Camp Grimley.

3) For one reason or another, almost every kid in the truck wasn't surprised that their parents would send them to a survival camp without telling them.

"Okay, so maybe I *did* make a mistake," I finally admitted. "Maybe Grimley is a survival camp. But so what? We're only going for three weeks. How bad could it be?"

Everyone turned to the thin kid with the toothpick behind his ear. Only he wasn't sitting at the end of the bench anymore. He'd stood up and was pulling on his backpack.

"What are you doing?" Josh asked him.

"Bailing," he answered.

"Where're you gonna go?" asked the chubby kid.

"Anywhere," said the kid with the toothpick. "As long as it's not Camp Grimley."

The truck stopped at a light. The kid with the toothpick jumped out and jogged into the woods beside the road.

The rest of the ride passed in silence as those of us left in the truck mulled over what lay ahead. It was midafternoon when the truck turned down a bumpy dirt road filled with rocks and potholes. For the next few hours we bounced and lurched deeper and deeper into a dark green, thickly wooded forest.

"When was the last time we saw another car?" the chubby kid wondered out loud.

"Hours ago," Andy answered forlornly.

"Talk about being in the middle of nowhere." Josh glowered at me as if it was all my fault.

"Let's try to look on the positive side," I said. "We'll probably learn about all kinds of things we never would have learned at the luxury camp. I bet this experience will make us better people."

"Get stuffed, Jake," Josh snapped. "Don't try to sell us on your mistake. You blew it. This is all your fault. End of sentence."

"All I'm saying is that we might as well try to make the best of it," I said.

The truck screeched to a stop and the crew-cut

driver came around to the back. "Okay, pork chops, get out."

We were in a clearing in the middle of the woods. In each corner of the clearing was a medium-size old-fashioned green Army tent. In the center of the clearing was a larger tent.

We climbed out. The driver started tossing our backpacks into a pile on the ground.

"Hey, take it easy!" Josh shouted at him. "I've got a brand-new tennis racket in there."

"A tennis racket?" the driver chuckled. "What are you gonna do with that?"

"Play tennis, what else?" Josh answered.

The driver just smiled to himself and threw another backpack onto the pile.

Meanwhile Andy and I looked around.

"I hate to say this, Josh," Andy said, "but I don't see any tennis courts."

"Gimme a break," Josh replied impatiently. "*This* isn't the camp. There's nothing here. This is just some stopping-off place. We probably have to hike from here."

Just then, the flaps of the big tent in the center of the clearing parted and a man stepped out carrying a clipboard. He looked like he was about our parents' age, only he was a lot more muscular than any of our fathers. Like the driver of the truck, he had a crew cut and was wearing an olive-colored T-shirt and camouflage pants. He was followed by a small group of people who looked like they might have been in college. I had a feeling they were our counselors.

A whistle hung around the man's neck. He placed it in his lips and blew. *Fweeeeet!*

Everyone turned and looked at him.

"If I could have your attention, boys and girls," he said. "My name is Cal McPhearsome and I run Camp Grimley."

He looked down at the clipboard and frowned. Then he looked back at the driver. "Hey, Dewey, how many did you pick up?"

"Twenty, sir," Dewey answered.

"I only count nineteen now," said Cal. "Looks like someone flew the coop. You know what to do."

"Right away, sir." Dewey hurried back to the truck and took off up the dirt road.

Cal McPhearsome turned to us. "In case you're wondering, kids. Dewey's job is to round up any of you who might entertain the notion of leaving camp early. He's darn good at it, too. We've only lost one camper in the past five years. And *no one* ever found him."

He paused and smiled. "Welcome to Camp Grimley."

PART TWO
THE ULTIMATE DRAG

8

The good news was that Andy, Josh, and I were all assigned to the same tent, along with the tall kid, whose name was Jeremy, and the chubby kid, whose name was Martin. The bad news was that our counselor, Ted, was from total weirdness. He was a big, bearish-looking guy with long blond hair halfway down his back. His bushy blond beard and mustache looked like they'd never been trimmed.

He was wearing a green T-shirt with the slogan "Think Like an Animal" on the back. His khaki shorts had extrabig pockets, and his hiking boots were worn-out and battered. In a quiver made from animal skins, he carried a bow made from a stick and some arrows with stone-tipped arrowheads.

"If you're wondering about my T-shirt," he said as he led us to our tent, "it reflects my philosophy of survival in the wilderness. You must become at one with nature. You have to learn to think like an animal."

Walking behind him, Josh rolled his eyes like he thought Ted was mental.

We followed him into the tent. Inside, it was dark and smelled musty.

"Any questions?" Ted asked.

"Yeah," said Josh. "Where do we sleep?"

"Anyplace you want," answered our counselor.

"I don't think you understand," Josh said. "Where are the beds? Where are the cubbies?"

"We sleep on the ground like the rest of nature's animals," Ted replied.

Andy's eyes widened. "On the ground?"

"What about a bathroom?" asked Martin, the short, chubby kid.

"The woods," said Ted.

"The woods?" Josh repeated in disbelief.

"I know we'll be eating dinner later, but I'm really hungry," said Jeremy, the tall kid. "Is there a camp canteen or a snack bar?"

"No snack bar or canteen," said Ted.

"What about a dining hall?" I asked.

"No dining hall," said Ted.

Josh turned pale. "No snack bar. No dining hall. Then what do we eat?"

"After tonight, you'll eat what nature provides," replied Ted. "The other counselors may disagree, but as far as I'm concerned, there's an

177

amazing amount of food in the wilderness. Wild game, and fish from the river. All kinds of berries and roots. And as a last resort, there's always edible tree bark and a wide variety of insects that are very high in protein."

Josh turned to me. He looked ill. "Did he say tree bark and insects?"

I nodded.

"Excuse me." Josh picked up his backpack. "I must be in the wrong place."

He marched out of the tent. Andy and I chased after him.

"Wait!" I said. "I know it's not exactly what we were hoping for."

"Talk about exaggeration," Josh groused.

"It's not really an exaggeration," Andy corrected him. "It's more of an understatement."

"We're not in school anymore, dimwit," Josh grumbled.

As we passed the big tent in the center of the clearing, the flap opened and Cal McPhearsome stepped out. He crossed his muscular arms and blocked Josh's path.

"Going somewhere?" he asked.

"You bet," Josh answered. "I'm thinking like an animal. Like a homing pigeon. I'm going home."

Cal nodded patiently. I had a feeling he'd heard this before. "And just how do you expect to get there?"

"I'll walk if I have to," Josh replied stubbornly.

"It's going to be dark in a few hours," Cal said. "Do you know what happens around here at night?"

Josh shook his head.

"Some pretty nasty critters come out," Cal said. "You've got your snakes, wolves, bobcats, and mosquitoes the size of your fist. Oh, and don't forget about the bears."

Josh swallowed nervously. "Bears?"

"Big bears," Cal said. "Know what we call campers who go out in the woods alone at night?"

Josh shook his head.

Cal grinned. "Grizzly bait."

9

Josh decided not to leave camp after all. A little while later, our tent joined the rest of the camp around a big fire where we ate our last "real" meal of franks and beans.

"For the next two weeks we'll learn everything we can about surviving in the wilderness," said Ted, who skipped dinner and ate carrot sticks and apples instead.

"How come you're having that stuff?" Andy asked him.

"I don't believe in eating processed foods," our counselor answered. "Apples are high in natural fiber, and carrots have vitamin A, which improves your night vision. That'll be important when we get to the Ultimate Challenge."

"The what?" asked Martin.

"You'll see," Ted replied mysteriously.

After dinner, Ted told us to collect pine branches and dry grass for bedding under our sleeping bags. The camp had no electricity and the tent had no light, so we lay in the dark.

"What are we supposed to do at night?" Andy asked.

"Most nights you'll be so tired you'll just want to sleep," Ted replied.

"But tonight we're awake," Josh said. "What about some entertainment?"

"All right," said Ted. "Ever hear of Uncle Remus?"

"Who's that?" asked Jeremy, the tall kid.

"Famous American folktale," answered Ted. "For hundreds of years before the invention of television, people entertained each other by telling stories. The Uncle Remus stories are about Brer Rabbit and his friends, Brer Bear and Brer Fox."

Josh rolled his eyes. "Sounds thrilling."

For the next hour, Ted told us the story of how Brer Rabbit tricked Brer Fox into throwing him in the brier patch. By the time our counselor finished, just about everyone was asleep, mostly from boredom. I was drifting off toward dreamland when Ted quietly got up, took his day pack, and crept out of the tent.

"Where do you think he's going?" I whispered to anyone in the tent who might still be awake.

"Probably to sleep on a *real* bed," Jeremy answered grumpily.

10

It felt like the middle of the night when Ted woke us. The tent was dark and the air was damp and cold.

"Rise and shine, guys, the sun's coming up," he said.

"So?" I yawned.

"Time to get into nature's rhythm," our counselor explained. "For the next three weeks we'll be diurnal animals. That's the opposite of nocturnal. We'll rise and set with the sun. See you outside."

Ted left the tent. When he opened the flap, I caught a glimpse of the dawn's gray light. Then the flap closed and it was dark again. None of us budged from our sleeping bags.

"Shouldn't we get up?" Martin asked.

"Maybe *you* should," Josh grumbled, "but I prefer to make like Brer Rabbit and luxuriate here in my comfortable bed of twigs and grass."

"Ted's going to be ticked off if we don't get up," Andy warned him.

"Ted can go jump in the lake," Josh replied.

"Since there's no lake around here," Andy pointed out, "that's a figure of speech."

"I wish I could figure out how to shut you up," Josh growled.

"I'm going to get up," said Jeremy. "I'm hungry. Maybe they'll have a decent breakfast."

He crawled out of his sleeping bag, pulled on some clothes, and left the tent.

"I'm going, too," said Martin. He got up and followed Jeremy.

Andy was the next to rise. "Might as well get up. I've been lying on a stick all night. It keeps poking me in the back."

He went outside, leaving Josh and me in the tent.

"What're you going to do, Jake?" Josh asked in the dim gray light.

"I hate to say it, but I'm hungry, too," I answered and pushed myself up. Like Andy, I'd had a hard time finding a comfortable position during the night. Sleeping on pine branches and dry grass might have been more comfortable than sleeping on the cold hard ground, but it wasn't a feather bed, either.

"Traitor," Josh griped as I left the tent.

Outside, the day was slowly growing brighter. The girl campers from the tent next to ours were also coming out. They were all wearing shorts and running shoes. One of them was the girl with the spiky black hair and lipstick. We'd learned that her name was Tara.

"Okay, Forest Runners, let's stretch," said their counselor. She was a stocky, blond lady with a crew cut and lots of earrings.

The girls from her tent groaned and exchanged woeful looks, but they started to stretch. Andy and I went over to Tara.

"What's the Forest Runner stuff?" Andy asked her.

"It's the name Morgan gave our tent," Tara answered while she bent down and tried to touch her toes.

"Who's Morgan?" I asked.

"My counselor," said Tara.

"Ready for an easy five-mile run?" Morgan asked the Forest Runners.

"Five miles?" Andy swallowed.

"Morgan says that physical fitness is the key to survival in the wilderness," Tara explained. "Guess that means we're gonna run a lot."

Andy and I watched as she jogged away and joined the rest of the Forest Runners.

"I'm glad I'm not in *that* tent," Andy whispered.

A counselor with thick glasses and a backpack bulging with gear came out of the third tent, followed by a bunch of yawning, bleary-eyed campers. They were all carrying knives or small hatchets.

"Okay, Techno-Wizards," the counselor announced cheerfully. "The first thing we're going to do is hone up on our sharpening skills. Or maybe we'll sharpen up our honing skills."

The campers from his tent groaned loudly to show they thought it was a lame joke. But just the same, they started to sharpen their tools.

"Can you believe they're called the Techno-Wizards?" Andy mumbled as he and I rejoined Ted and the rest of our team. "Is that a dumb name or what?"

"They can choose whatever name they want," Ted explained. "Their counselor, Philip, takes the technical approach."

The flap of the fourth tent opened and out staggered a scary-looking counselor whose long unruly hair was held back by a red bandanna around his forehead. He was wearing a faded denim jacket with the sleeves torn off, black pants, and heavy black boots.

He yawned without bothering to cover his mouth and gave the counselors from the other tents a stony look. Then he spit on the ground and went back into his own tent.

"That guy looks like he belongs in a motorcycle gang, not in a survival camp," Josh quipped.

"So what's his philosophy of survival?" Andy asked.

"Axel?" Ted shook his head. "You don't want to know."

11

Ted told us to sit in a circle and cross our legs. Andy and I frowned but lowered ourselves to the dew-covered ground.

We'd just sat down when Josh came out of the tent rubbing his eyes. When he saw us sitting in a circle he grinned. "Aw, how cute. We're playing our first camp game — duck, duck, goose."

"Have a seat, Josh," Ted replied and then said to the rest of us, "place your hands on your knees. Straighten your backs, close your eyes."

"Why?" asked Josh.

"Because," Ted replied, "we begin each day by meditating on the wonders of nature."

"Talk about wonders," Jeremy said, "I'm wondering when we might get some breakfast."

"Later," Ted answered. "Now breathe deeply through your noses. Relax. Try to absorb the wilderness energy."

Ah-choo! Josh sneezed. "Sorry. Guess I absorbed the wilderness pollen instead."

The rest of us chuckled.

"Focus, boys," Ted said without opening his eyes.

We all sat on the cold ground, meditating.

"Uh, excuse me for interrupting, Ted," Martin said, "but what are we supposed to do with the wilderness energy once we've absorbed it?"

"Don't worry," Ted replied. "Your body will know what to do."

"My body knows it wants to eat breakfast," said Jeremy.

"Mine, too," agreed Andy.

"Hush!" Ted said sternly. "This is serious."

We all got quiet but not for long. Someone's stomach started to rumble. I opened one eye and saw Josh grin. The rumbling grew louder. Now everyone except Ted had opened one eye and was grinning.

"Earthquake!" Josh cried.

Everyone started to laugh.

Ted opened his eyes and looked really annoyed.

"Hey, come on, Ted," Andy chuckled. "It's funny."

But Ted didn't smile. "You won't think it's funny two weeks from now."

12

Ted quit trying to get us to meditate and stood up.

"We go single file," he said and started toward the woods.

"What did you say happens two weeks from now?" Andy asked as we followed him.

"The Ultimate Challenge," Ted answered.

"What's that?" asked Martin.

"A situation where you'll be expected to use your wilderness skills," said our counselor.

"So, it's like a test or something?" I guessed.

"You could say that," Ted replied. "Only it's not like any test you've ever taken before."

"Why not?" asked Josh.

"Because it's a survival test," Ted said.

"What happens if you don't pass?" Martin asked.

"Uh, you have to come back again next year?" Andy guessed.

"In that case, we better pass," said Josh.

Ted didn't say a thing. He just walked deeper into the woods. I noticed that, unlike the rest of us, our counselor walked by placing his toe down first and then his heel.

"How come you walk like that?" I asked.

"It's the quiet way," Ted answered. "To stalk prey."

Behind him, Josh started to prance on his toes like a ballerina. The rest of us clamped our hands over our mouths to keep from laughing.

We came to a brook. Above us, shafts of sunlight streamed down through the breaks in the treetops. It felt good on our skin, but I could hear lots of stomachs grumbling hungrily, mine included.

"I sure hope this leads to a McDonald's," Andy said as we followed Ted along the brook.

"I could really go for pancakes," said Martin.

"With a shake and side orders of hash browns, sausage, and cornbread," added Jeremy.

Ted stopped by a bush and plucked off some red berries. "Try these."

We each put a few in our mouths. Mine tasted sweet but tart. "What is it?"

"Wild raspberries," Ted said. He turned to Josh, who was the only one among us who hadn't tried a berry. "Want one?"

Josh shook his head. "I don't like fresh fruit."

"I feel a lot of negative energy coming from you, Josh," Ted said.

189

"You can thank Jake for that," Josh answered bitterly.

Breakfast wasn't from McDonald's. It was from the brook. Ted taught us how to make spears from tree branches. Then he started a fire with a bow drill and a fire board while the rest of us waded into the brook and speared fish.

I wasn't a big fan of fish, but by the time we'd caught enough for a meal, the sun was high overhead and I was starving. Everyone ate the fish. Everyone, that is, except Josh.

"I don't like fish," he grumbled.

"No offense or anything, Ted," said Jeremy. "But how come you don't eat normal food?"

"This *is* normal food," Ted replied. "This is what nature provides. The junk *you* eat is abnormal food. It's processed and filled with chemicals, preservatives, and synthetic growth hormones."

"But at least that stuff *tastes* good," said Josh as he finally gave in and nibbled on a little piece of fish.

"You'll be surprised how fast you'll get to like this food," Ted said.

Jeremy took a bite and grimaced. "Sure, when you're starving to death *anything* tastes good."

13

We spent the rest of the day learning how to tie knots, find water, and build a shelter out of pine branches and reeds. As evening approached, we speared more fish and gathered blueberries for dinner.

Tired and aching from the day's work, we headed back through the woods toward camp. We were dirty and hungry, and our hands were scraped and full of splinters.

"I want to go to a different camp!" Josh wailed.

"Try to think positively," Ted urged him. "You're going to stay here and get tough. You're going to learn to become at one with nature."

"I'm already at one with nature," Josh replied. "I just wish I could make like a tree and leave."

Once again, our stomachs were grumbling hungrily.

"Earthquake!" Martin called out.

This time, nobody laughed.

As we got closer to the camp, we could smell the scent of smoke.

"Smells like someone's cooking," Andy said.

"Smells great," I said.

"It's . . . it's steak!" Jeremy gasped. Suddenly he broke out of our single-file line and raced ahead through the forest.

The rest of us gave Ted desperate, pleading looks, but our counselor shook his head.

We reached the edge of camp and were stunned to see the other campers sitting outside their tents eating dinner.

"How come they get real food and we don't?" I asked.

"What you eat is up to your counselor," Ted replied. He pointed at Morgan's tent, where the Forest Runners were sitting around a big pot of spaghetti. Their hair was damp with perspiration and their sweat-soaked T-shirts clung to their bodies. They had obviously spent the day running and exercising.

"Do you realize that spaghetti is made with processed flour?" Ted asked. "And that tomato sauce is full of preservatives?"

"I'd kill for some preservatives," Andy moaned.

Ted ignored him and pointed at Philip's tent. Heavy backpacks loaded with compasses, butane stoves, and orange two-man tents lay on the ground. The Techno-Wizards were eating lumpy-looking foods out of plastic bags.

"They're eating freeze-dried junk," Ted grumbled with distaste. "That stuff is filled with nitrates."

"I'd give my left hand for some nitrates!" Martin cried.

The smell of grilling steaks was coming from Axel's tent. His campers were eating super-rare steaks with bloodred insides. Bright red steak juice ran down their chins as they gnawed hungrily. I wondered what they'd done all day. A tree nearby was covered with freshly gouged initials, and next to the tent lay a bunch of thick sticks that resembled crude baseball bats.

Jeremy was following Axel around, begging for a piece of steak. Axel didn't say a word. He just gave him that stony look. Finally, when Jeremy wouldn't stop begging, Axel pushed him to the ground.

"Hey!" Andy gasped. "Why'd he do that? They've got extra steaks on the grill. They could spare some."

"Axel's not going to share," Ted said.

"Why not?" I asked.

Our counselor just shrugged and didn't answer.

Jeremy trudged back from Axel's tent. "I can't believe he wouldn't give me some steak."

"You don't want that stuff," Ted said. "Red meat's full of cholesterol and fat. Soda's full of processed sugar. All that stuff'll kill you."

"So what?" Josh moaned. "Another two weeks of fish and berries and we'll all be dead anyway."

PART THREE
THE ULTIMATE DECISION

14

"This is the day we've all been waiting for — the Ultimate Challenge," Cal McPhearsome said. "Starting today, only one law applies — survival of the fittest."

It was just after dawn and we were gathered outside our tents. It amazed me how the campers on each team had started to look more and more like their counselors over the past two weeks.

In the misty grayness, Morgan's Forest Runners were all wearing warm-ups and sweatbands around their foreheads. Philip's Techno-Wizards each carried a heavy backpack loaded with gear.

And this was the first time I'd seen Axel's Vulture team up before noon. Like Axel, they were all wearing heavy boots, black jeans, and denim jackets with the sleeves torn off. One of them was Ron, the thin kid who'd jumped off the truck on the first day. As usual he had a toothpick in his mouth and that stony, silent look he'd learned from Axel. We'd nicknamed him Toothpick.

"At noon today your teams will be air-dropped into the wilderness fifty miles from here," Cal announced. "Your job will be to find your way back to camp. The first team that makes it back gets three pizzas with all the toppings they want, plus three big bottles of soda and three big bags of potato chips."

Murmurs broke out among the campers. By now, the Forest Runners were as sick of spaghetti and the Techno-Wizards as sick of freeze-dried scrambled eggs as we were of fish and berries.

"I'd kill for pizza," Josh muttered in despair. I'd never seen him so thin and gaunt. Then again, all of us from the Weed Eaters' tent were thin and gaunt.

"Remember," Cal went on. "Only the winners get pizza. Between now and noon your counselors will announce which of you will go on the challenge. Don't forget, this isn't a game. It's survival. We live in a take-no-prisoners world here. What's our camp motto?"

"Show no mercy!" some of Axel's Vultures shouted. The rest of us were too busy whispering to each other. Josh turned to Ted. "What did he mean, you'll announce who's going on the Ultimate Challenge? Aren't we all going?"

Ted shook his head. "Each counselor takes his best three campers. The others stay behind."

"And do what?" Andy asked.

Ted shrugged. "Whatever they want."

"What about food?" asked Jeremy.

"The camp will supply it," answered Ted.

Josh blinked with astonishment. "You mean, two of us *won't* have to go on the Ultimate Challenge? We can just hang around here and eat?"

Ted nodded. "You'll be left behind. You won't have the satisfaction of putting what you've learned to the test."

Josh looked like he was ready to jump for joy. "Believe me, that's one satisfaction I can live without!"

Ted gave him a frustrated look. "Why can't you have a positive attitude, Josh?"

"I am positive," Josh protested. "Positive that I don't want to go on the Ultimate Challenge! So who's going and who's staying?"

"I haven't decided yet," Ted answered. "I'll let you know."

Then he went back into the tent.

15

The Weed Eaters sat in a circle outside our tent and waited for Ted to make his decision. We were dirty and skinny. Everyone's stomach growled loudly.

"If I have to go into the woods and eat berries for another week, I'm gonna die," Jeremy moaned.

"If I have to listen to Ted tell another dumb story about Brer Rabbit faking out Brer Fox, I'll go nuts," complained Josh.

While we waited, we watched the other teams get ready for the challenge. Morgan's Forest Runners loaded their backpacks with boxes of spaghetti. Outside the Techno-Wizards' tent, Philip gave each of his campers a shiny new compass. Axel's Vultures had gone back into their tent to prepare in secret.

"Everyone else is getting ready, and meanwhile we're just sitting here doing nothing," Andy moped.

"You know what Ted would say," replied Martin. "We should be meditating and becoming at one with nature. That's how he wants us to get ready."

Josh shook his head woefully. "I don't want to go. Cal said two of us wouldn't have to. I'd do anything if he'd pick me to stay behind."

"We all would," Martin said. "Boy, what I wouldn't give to be somewhere else right now."

"Or *someone* else," quipped Jeremy.

In the silent moment that followed, Josh leveled his gaze at me. I could almost see the lightbulb go off in his brain. He pushed himself up.

"Let's take a walk, Jake," he said.

"Where?" Andy asked.

"Nowhere you're going," Josh replied.

"Wait a minute!" Andy gasped. "You're up to something. I can tell."

"Forget it," Josh said. "Jake and I are just gonna talk."

"Not without me, you're not." Andy got up.

The three of us strolled into the woods behind the tents. I already knew what Josh had in mind.

"The answer is totally no," I said.

"Listen, Jake, I've been your friend for a long time," Josh said anxiously. "I've helped you out of some seriously harsh jams. I wouldn't even be here if it wasn't for you. You owe me."

Andy's jaw dropped as he realized what Josh was talking about. "The mini-DITS!"

Shhhh! Josh and I pressed our fingers against our lips.

"You don't want someone to hear, jerkhead," Josh hissed.

"Jake, you can't help Josh and not me," Andy gasped. "If he gets out of going, so do I!"

"I'm not switching anyone," I said. "I don't even know if the mini-DITS works. Dirksen's never tried it on anyone."

"I'm gonna be the first guinea pig," insisted Josh.

"I'll be the second," added Andy.

"It doesn't make sense, guys," I said. "Who are you going to switch with? Who do you know who's definitely *not* going on the Ultimate Challenge?"

Andy's shoulders sagged. "Jake's right. We don't know who's going and who's not. We could switch with someone and still wind up going."

Josh stared off into the woods. A smile slowly crept across his lips. It was the first time he'd smiled since we arrived at Camp Grimley. "There's a way," he said. "And it'll guarantee that neither Andy or I will go."

16

Josh turned to me. "We're not going to switch with anyone. *You* are, Jake."

"Me?" I scowled. "How would that stop Ted from picking you for the Ultimate Challenge?"

"Because you'll switch with Ted," Josh explained. "And then you'll decide that Andy and I aren't going."

"That's right!" Andy cried. "Jake, you have to do it!"

"But if I switch with Ted, that means I definitely have to go," I said.

"So?" Josh asked.

"Why should I have to go if you don't?" I asked.

"You want one good reason?" Josh answered. *"Because this is all your fault!* We wouldn't be at this stupid camp if it wasn't for you. We wouldn't be dirty and hungry and miserable."

"Maybe I made a mistake," I admitted. "But it was an honest mistake. I didn't do it on purpose."

"Doesn't matter," Josh countered. "This is the

200

only way you can possibly make up for it. Right, Andy?"

Andy nodded in agreement. Deep inside, I knew they were right. It *was* all my fault. If only I hadn't gotten the names of the camps mixed up!

"Okay, I'll do it," I finally agreed. "Or at least I'll try. You guys are going to have to come up with a way to trick Ted into switching bodies with me."

Josh grinned. "Piece of cake."

"Ahem." Andy cleared his throat. "Given the circumstances, I think you mean piece of *fish*."

17

You can't live in a tent with someone for two weeks and not learn a few of his secrets. We knew that when Ted went out for his nightly strolls he always took a Walkman with tapes of a band called Phluke. My friends and I didn't know much about that band, but Martin did because he had a friend who was a "Phlukehead."

"It's like this cult," he'd told us. "They trade tapes of concerts. The New Year's Eve concerts are real favorites."

Josh, Andy, and I went back to camp and into the tent. Ted was inside, sitting cross-legged, still trying to decide who was going to go on the Ultimate Challenge.

"You really have a tape of the 1992 New Year's Eve show?" Josh asked me with a wink.

"Oh, uh, yeah," I said. "I sure do."

"You have it here?" Josh asked, pretending to get excited. "On your Walkman?"

"Yup." I glanced out of the corner of my eye and noticed that Ted was giving us a curious look.

"Oh, man, I have to hear it!" Josh cried.

I went over to my backpack and started to open it.

"What New Year's Eve show?" Ted asked.

"It's nothing," Josh said. "Just this band we like."

"What band?" asked Ted.

"Phluke," Andy said. "Most of our friends think they're lame, but we're really into them."

Ted smiled knowingly. "Well, I've got news for you. There are no tapes of the 1992 New Year's Eve show because there was no New Year's Eve show that year."

Andy and Josh gave me a panicked look.

"Oh, uh, sure there was," I bluffed. "They, er, just didn't play at the regular place."

"You mean, the Ocean Palace?" Ted said.

"Uh, right," I said. "They played, uh, somewhere else."

"That must have been the Seaside Ballroom," Ted said to himself. "But everybody would have known if Phluke played there."

"It, uh, was just for their friends," Josh said.

Ted got up. "I have to hear this."

"Sure!" Josh smiled. "Jake, get out your Walkman."

I took out the mini-DITS.

"That's the strangest-looking Walkman I've ever seen," Ted said. "Why are there two sets of headphones?"

"It's made specially for audiodigital spiritual tape," Josh quickly ad-libbed. "And it comes with two sets of headphones because it's for people who want to share the experience."

"I've never heard of anything like that," Ted said, but he took the headphones anyway. "Still, I have to hear this. I can't believe it's a real tape."

"Uh, you wouldn't mind if Jake listens, too, would you?" Josh asked.

Ted suddenly frowned. "Wait a minute, I thought *you* were the one who wanted to hear it. What's going on?"

Josh turned to me and made another face, as if begging me to come up with an explanation. But this time I couldn't think of one.

"There's just one special part Josh wants to listen to," Andy piped up. "Jake's going to find it for him."

"Oh, okay." Ted put the headphones on.

Josh turned to me. "Well, what are you waiting for?"

I sighed reluctantly and slid on the headphones. Josh picked up the mini-DITS and pushed the button.

Whump!

18

There are some things you never get used to. Switching bodies is definitely one of them. When I opened my eyes I was lying on the dirt floor of the tent. I brought my hands to my face and felt Ted's broad, bushy beard. It was like the time I switched bodies with Santa Claus.

"What is this?" I heard my voice ask. Only I wasn't the one who'd asked it. I looked around and saw Ted in my body staring at his hands.

"We switched you," Josh said.

Usually the people you switch bodies with wig out in surprise and disbelief. But Ted in my body calmly stared across the tent at me in his body. Then he pointed at the mini-DITS.

"I assume this is what switched us," he said.

"That's right," said Andy. "How come you're not totally wigged?"

"Well, to tell you the truth, I've never been a big fan of the human body," Ted answered. "The fact that we can switch sort of confirms what I've believed all along. Can you switch us back?"

"When we want to," Josh said.

"And when will that be?" asked Ted in my body.

"When the Ultimate Challenge is over," Andy informed him.

An odd smile appeared on Ted's lips. "No kidding? And what did I do to deserve this?"

"You never let us have anything decent to eat," Josh said angrily. "Maybe, if you'd let us eat better, we'd be more willing to help you out of this ridiculous situation. But *noooooooooo*, you had to make us eat fish and berries and sleep on the cold hard ground and —"

Ted in my body wasn't listening. Smiling broadly, he turned to me. "Now that you're in my body, you'll have to lead the Weed Eaters on the Ultimate Challenge."

"I know." I nodded sadly and felt Ted's long hair wiggle up and down my back.

"You won't stand a chance," said Ted in my body. "No, I take that back. You have *one* chance. I know secrets — places where you can find food and water, shortcuts, ways to avoid being ambushed. I could write it all down for you."

"Write it down?" Josh repeated, confused. "Why?"

"Because," Ted in my body announced joyfully, "now that we've switched bodies, there's no way in the world I'm going with you!"

19

"**B**ut you *have* to go," Josh insisted.

"Why?" asked Ted in my body.

"Because the whole reason we switched you and Jake was so that he could let Josh and me stay behind," Andy explained.

Ted shook my head and smiled. "Sorry. Maybe *one* of you will stay behind, but not both of you."

Josh turned to me in Ted's body. "Tell him he has to go, Jake."

But before I could say anything, Ted in my body pointed a stern finger at me. "Here's what will happen if you try to take me," he warned in an ominous tone. "As soon as we're in the wilderness, I'll leave you. Don't forget, Jake, I *know* the wilderness. I can live out there for months with just my bare hands. And without me, you won't stand a chance. The only hope you have is to learn my secrets. But I won't tell them to you unless you promise not to take me."

"But if you're so great at living in the wilderness, why don't you want to go?" Andy asked.

"Uh . . ." Ted in my body seemed flustered for a moment. "Er . . . because once we're out there, it's . . . uh . . . a group effort. And there's no way I would want to depend on a bunch of bozos like you."

"Are you *sure* that's the reason?" I asked.

"Sure I'm sure," Ted in my body insisted.

"Talk about negative energy," Josh mumbled.

Ted in my body looked back at me. "I've given you the choice, Jake. Take my secrets into the wilderness and you'll have a chance. Take me and you've got about as much hope as a turtle crossing a highway at rush hour."

I tried to rub my chin and think, but my chin was covered with all of Ted's beard hair. I turned to my friends. "I hate to say this, guys, but it's starting to sound like an offer I can't refuse."

"But that means either Andy or I will have to go with you!" Josh gasped.

"I know," I said.

Josh turned to Andy. "Then *you* should go."

"Why me?" Andy asked.

"Because I won't make it!" Josh cried. "If I have to eat one more meal of fish and berries I'll go straight off the deep end."

"Well, so will I!" Andy shot back.

"Shoot for it, guys," suggested Ted in my body.

"Good idea!" Josh said. "Odds!"

"Evens!" said Andy.

They faced each other and each drew back a fist, preparing to shoot.

"Wait a minute," Josh said. "Let's make it two out of three."

"Three out of five," Andy countered.

"Four out of six," said Josh.

"No, four out of *seven*," Andy corrected him.

"Five out of eight," said Josh.

"Six out of ten," Andy said.

"Seven out of thirteen," insisted Josh.

I turned to Ted in my body. "What about those secrets?"

"Let's go get something to write on," he replied.

"Nine out of seventeen," Andy was saying as we left the tent.

"Ten out of nineteen," yelled Josh.

Ted in my body and I in his left the tent . . . and came face-to-face with Axel.

The Vultures' counselor was dressed in black, with a black bandanna around his head and camouflage paint smeared on his face. He blocked my path and didn't say a word. He just glared at me with that stony expression.

"Uh, what's up?" I asked, nervously.

"Feeling worried, Teddy Bear?" Axel growled.

"What about?" I asked.

"You know what about," said Toothpick, who'd come with his counselor and was also dressed in black. "Axel told us what happened last year. If I were you, I'd quit the Ultimate Challenge now."

"Why?" I asked.

Axel didn't answer. He just glowered at me with that stony look.

"Okay, boys, break it up." It was Cal McPhearsome. "Save it for the wilderness."

Axel narrowed his eyes menacingly at me, then stomped away. I turned to the head of the camp. "What can I do for you, Mr. McPhearsome?"

Ted in my body pulled me aside. "Call him Cal," he hissed. "Remember, you're in my body now."

"Right." I turned to Cal again.

"Time's running out, Ted," Cal said to me. "You have to decide who you're taking with you."

Cal left. Martin and Jeremy were sitting outside our tent, looking pale and scared. They stared at me with fearful eyes, as if dreading the thought that I in Ted's body might pick them to go.

"Hey, don't look like that, guys," said Ted in my body. "It won't be that bad."

"Oh, really, Jake?" Martin answered. "Has Ted told you why Axel's Vultures look more like assassins than survivalists?"

I gave Ted in my body a curious look, but of course he couldn't explain in front of them.

"We won't stand a chance against them," whimpered Jeremy.

"What are you talking about?" I asked.

"Get off it, Ted," Martin replied unhappily.

210

"Stop pretending that you don't know. This is what the Ultimate Challenge is all about. It's not just about surviving in the wilderness. It's about surviving against your fellow campers as well. That's why they keep talking about how our lives are going to depend on each other. That's why the camp motto is 'Show no mercy.'"

I gave Ted in my body a questioning look.

"Let's go inside," he said.

Inside our tent, Josh and Andy were still shooting to see who would stay behind.

"Once! Twice! Three! Shoot!" They each swung an arm forward and held out one finger.

"Even!" Andy cried. "That's thirty-seven to thirty-four!"

"What are you shooting to?" I asked.

"A hundred and fifty-one out of three hundred," Andy said.

"And no do-overs," added Josh.

"Force field," confirmed Andy, holding back his hand again. "Ready?"

"Ready," Josh said.

"Once! Twice! Three! Shoot!"

Josh stuck out one finger again, but this time Andy stuck out two.

"Odds!" Josh grinned. "Thirty-seven to thirty-five!"

Ted in my body and I huddled in a corner of the tent.

"So what's the story with Axel?" I whispered.

Ted in my body shrugged. "Things got a little nasty during last year's Ultimate Challenge," he whispered back. "And I —"

"Uh, Ted?" Before he could continue, we were interrupted by Martin. "Think I could speak to you in private?"

"Not right now," I answered.

"But it's important," Martin insisted. "I really have to talk to you."

I gave Ted in my body a questioning look.

"Go ahead," he said. "I'll tell you the rest of the story later."

Leaving Ted in my body in the tent, Martin and I went outside. Martin glanced around to make sure no one could hear us.

"Uh, listen, Ted," he said in a low voice. "I know I'm supposed to *want* the Ultimate Challenge, but to be totally honest, I really don't. I'm really scared. I never wanted to come to this dumb camp in the first place."

He blinked and wiped a tear out of his eye. "I mean, I'm scared of the wilderness, I'm scared of the animals, and I'm totally freaked by Axel and those Vultures."

More tears rolled down Martin's cheeks. "I'm sorry, Ted. I'm a wilderness failure. I'm not at one with nature. I'm at one with wimpdom. I wish I wasn't, but I can't help it. I really can't go. I know I'll freeze up. I'm really, really terrified."

He started to sob and shake.

"Hey, that's okay." I put my, I mean, Ted's hand on Martin's shoulder and tried to reassure him. Martin was really bawling now. I could feel him trembling. He wasn't kidding when he said he was scared. This wasn't like Josh threatening to go off the deep end. This was serious.

Martin fell to his knees, clasped his hands, and looked up at me with wet, red-rimmed eyes. "Please, Ted! I'm begging you, please don't make me go! Please! I beg you!"

20

How could I say no? Deep down inside I knew that Andy and Josh would be able to cope with the Ultimate Challenge better than Martin. They wouldn't like it, and they'd probably hate me for the rest of my life, but at least they'd survive. Martin, on the other hand, would probably wig out and spend the rest of his life in a loony bin.

"Okay, Martin," I said. "You don't have to go."

"Oh, thank you, Ted!" Martin wrapped his arms around my knees. "Thank you so much!"

"Ted?" Cal McPhearsome called from the front of the tent. "Ted, you here?"

"Coming!" I called back, and gently eased myself away from Martin.

I went around the tent. Cal was waiting with his lips pursed together pensively. "Take a look." He handed me a white T-shirt. A message was scrawled on it in black marker:

Dear Ted,
I can't do it. Sorry to cop out on you.
By the time you read this, I'll be long gone.
— Jeremy

"He's probably headed out on the road," Cal said. "I've sent Dewey to find him. But the helicopter's due here in half an hour. He won't be back by then."

"So Jeremy can't go on the Ultimate Challenge," I said.

"That's right, Ted," Cal said. "You'll have to choose from the other boys. All the other counselors have picked their teams. It's time you picked yours."

Just then the tent flaps opened and Josh and Andy came out, followed by Ted in my body.

"You cheated!" Andy cried angrily.

"Did not!" Josh yelled back.

"Did too!" Andy insisted. "You held back on the last shot and waited to see what I'd shoot. I formally declare the whole shoot-out null and void!"

"You can't!" Josh shouted. "We agreed no do-overs, force field, remember?"

"That was *before* you cheated!" Andy yelled.

"Face it, Andy," Josh said. "You lost a hundred and fifty to a hundred and fifty-one."

"No way!" Andy yelled. "It doesn't count!"

"What's this all about, boys?" Cal asked.

Josh and Andy instantly clammed up.

Our counselor in my body stepped between them and looked at me.

"So, Ted, have you decided who you're taking?" he asked.

"Funny you should ask that, Jake," Cal said to him. "Ted's just about to tell me."

The time had come. Josh and Andy both stared at me with silent, pleading expressions. Ted in my body narrowed his eyes menacingly.

"Who's going with you on the Ultimate Challenge, Ted?" Cal asked.

I took a deep breath and let it out slowly. "Andy, Josh, and . . . Jake."

21

Josh's and Andy's mouths fell open and their eyes bulged out.

"What!?" Andy gasped.

"Some friend you are!" Josh sniffed.

"Your counselor is not supposed to be your friend," Cal informed him. "He's supposed to be your leader. You should be honored that he chose you for the Ultimate Challenge."

Josh spun toward Cal, and for a moment I feared that he was going to tell Cal exactly how he felt about the Ultimate Challenge. But he managed to hold his tongue.

Meanwhile, Ted in my body gave me a lethal stare.

"Okay, then," said Cal. "It's settled. Now you better get ready. You don't have much time." He moved to the Forest Runners' tent.

As soon as Cal was out of earshot, Andy and Josh got into my face.

"How could you do this to me?" Josh demanded hotly.

"I had no choice," I tried to explain. "I couldn't take one of you and leave the other. It wouldn't be fair."

"Why not?" Andy and Josh asked at the same time.

"Come on, guys, put yourself in my shoes," I said.

"If I was in your shoes I wouldn't even be at this dumb camp," Josh seethed. "I'd be at that luxury camp watching TV and eating Big Macs."

"And playing video games," Andy added with a pout.

"Go in the tent and get ready, boys," Ted in my body ordered.

Josh spun around and wrinkled his nose. "What'd you say?"

"I said, go in the tent," repeated Ted in my body.

The next thing I knew, Josh grabbed him by the collar of his T-shirt. "Let's get one thing straight, wuss. As long as you're in Jake's body, we don't have to listen to you. So bug off!"

Josh gave Ted in my body a shove and sent him reeling backward.

"That's showing him," Andy cheered. "So what do you want to do now, Josh?"

Josh looked around and scratched his head. "I guess we better go in the tent and get ready."

He pushed open the flap and went in. Andy frowned, then went in, too.

That left me, and Ted in my body. Ted glared at me. "I told you that if you picked me I'd leave you in the wilderness."

"I couldn't help it," I tried to explain. "Martin's wigging out and Jeremy ran away. Josh, Andy, and you are the only ones left."

Ted started to rub his chin, then frowned when he didn't feel any beard because he was in my body.

"Fine," he said. "But now that Josh and Andy are going, you might as well give me back my body."

He was right. The only reason I'd agreed to switch was so that Josh and Andy wouldn't have to go on the Ultimate Challenge. But now that they were going, there was no reason for me to be in Ted's body.

Or was there?

"If I give your body back, you'll definitely leave us in the wilderness," I said.

"Uh, no I won't," Ted in my body promised.

"I don't believe you," I said.

Ted narrowed my eyes angrily. "Okay, then I'll leave you *anyway*."

PART FOUR
THE ULTIMATE
CHALLENGE

22

"All right, men, listen up!" Cal shouted above the rumble of the helicopter as it skimmed over the vast and endless green treetops. All four teams were huddled in the open cargo bay of the chopper. As I held on tight and felt the helicopter vibrate, I watched the sun in the sky to our left.

"Each team will get one of these." Cal held up a small gray device that looked like a GameBoy. "It's a Computerized Pinpoint Positioner, or CPP. Your counselor will carry it. It emits a homing beacon so that we can track you down in case you really mess up. Now remember, it's for emergencies only. Your counselor knows that he's not supposed to use it for anything else."

Cal handed out the CPPs. Since I was in Ted's body, he gave one to me. As I put it in my day pack, I couldn't help noticing that when Axel got his, he shared a quick wink with Toothpick.

"We'll be dropping you off in a few minutes," Cal shouted. "Each team will start about a mile apart, but equidistant from the camp. The Vultures go first."

The helicopter slowed down and started to hover over a small clearing. Cal tossed a rope out of the helicopter bay.

"Show no mercy!" each Vulture shouted as he rappelled to the ground.

Axel was the last to go. He turned to me and bared his teeth in a snarl, revealing a glinting gold tooth. "*Hasta la vista*, Teddy Bear," he growled, then grabbed a rope and rappelled out of sight.

The next team off was the Techno-Wizards. Each of them clutched his new compass tightly. The third team to rappel out of the helicopter was the Forest Runners. Finally the Weed Eaters was the only team left.

As we got ready to slide down to the ground, Cal cleared his throat. "I might as well tell you that we took bets last night, and your team is the one everyone expects to come in last. I'd like to think that you'll surprise me, but frankly, I don't see how."

Josh and Andy exchanged a miserable look. Ted in my body just crouched in a corner and sneered at all of us. The helicopter started to hover. We pulled on small day packs with first aid kits in them. Ted in my body was the first to rappel. Then Josh and Andy went. As I grabbed the rope, I turned to Cal.

"Thanks for those words of confidence, sir."

23

I rappelled out of the chopper to the ground below. Andy and Josh were looking around at the thick forest with worried expressions on their faces.

Suddenly I heard a zipping sound behind me. I spun around, but I was too late. Ted in my body had gotten into my day pack and pulled out the CPP.

"This is your last chance," he warned. "Give my body back, and I'll help you guys. Don't give it back, and I'm out of here. And I'm taking *this* with me." He held up the CPP.

"If he takes the CPP, we're toast!" Andy cried. "We'll never find our way back, and Cal won't be able to find us, either!"

"You have to switch with him," Josh urged me.

A voice in my head told me not to do it. "No," I said.

"What?" Josh cried. "Have you gone psycho?"

"Please switch bodies, Jake," Andy begged. *"Please!"*

I shook my head.

"Have it your way," Ted smirked as he stuck the CPP in his pocket. "You know, nature's funny. One minute she's beautiful; the next minute she's filled with danger." He adjusted the straps of his pack. "I'd like to say it's been nice knowing you, boys, but it hasn't." He started to leave the clearing.

"Wait!" Josh cried.

Ted in my body stopped. "What?"

"Take us with you. *Please!*" Josh begged. He pointed at me in Ted's body. "If you leave us here with him, we'll die."

Ted in my body actually pursed his lips as if he was considering it. "Give me one good reason why I should take you."

"Because we're innocent," Josh yelped. "We didn't want to come here, either."

"So?" said Ted in my body.

"So . . . we could help you," Andy said.

Ted in my body scowled. "Help me? How? You're the worst students I've ever had."

"Well, maybe we can't help you *in* the wilderness," Andy said. "But we can help you when you get out."

Ted in my body continued to scowl.

"He's right," Josh said, following Andy's lead. "Like we can help you . . . uh . . . program a VCR."

"And order at the drive-thru window at fast-food places," said Andy.

"And we know all the secret codes to video games," added Josh.

"And how to get gum out of bubble-gum machines without paying," said Andy.

Ted in my body looked at my friends like they were crazy, then he turned away and started into the woods.

"Wait!" Andy yelled.

Again Ted in my body stopped. *"Now* what?"

"At least let us have the CPP," Andy begged.

"No." Ted turned toward the woods.

"Wait!" Josh cried.

This time Ted in my body didn't stop.

"Please take us!" Andy called.

Ted in my body disappeared among the trees.

Josh cupped his hands around his mouth and shouted, "Gee, thanks a lot!"

"Yeah," Andy yelled, "some friend you are."

"I hope you sink in quicksand!" Josh yelled.

"Or get eaten by a bear!" added Andy.

"Or bitten by a snake!" shouted Josh.

"Or . . . all of the above!" Andy shouted.

They stopped and listened. I guess they were hoping that Ted would change his mind and come back.

But all we heard was a bird chirp and the faint rustle of leaves in the light breeze.

Ted in my body was gone.

Josh and Andy glared at me in Ted's body.

"This is all your fault, Jake!" Andy yelled.

"Yeah!" cried Josh. "Now we're gonna die!"

"I'm never gonna learn to drive," Andy cried.

"I'm never gonna get to shave," added Josh.

"Or vote!" said Andy.

Josh made a face. "Who cares about that?"

"Hey, come on, guys," I said. "It's not that bad."

"Are you crazy?" Josh cried. "We're stuck deep in the wilderness about a million miles from everything. We don't have food, water, a place to sleep, or a weapon to defend ourselves against bears and snakes. This is worse than bad. It's the ultimate nightmare horribility!"

Andy frowned. "The *what*?"

"Horribility," Josh repeated.

"There's no such word," Andy said.

"Sure there is," said Josh. "Possible, horrible; possibility, horribility."

Andy shook his head. "No way."

"We can survive this," I said calmly.

"How?" Josh and Andy asked at the same time.

"We just have to stay cool and use everything we've learned," I said.

Josh and Andy looked at each other.

"In that case," began Josh.

"It's even worse than we thought!" cried Andy.

226

24

"**B**eing negative isn't going to help," I said.

"Look who's talking," smirked Josh. "Inside that hairy body is Jake Sherman, the great outdoorsman. Just because you're in Ted's body and you have a beard doesn't mean you know anything about the wilderness."

"Maybe I do," I said.

"Can you get us out of here?" Andy asked hopefully.

I looked around. The small clearing we were in was surrounded by thick, dark forest that looked as if it had never been disturbed. You could tell by the delicate moss growing on the fallen logs and by the small, frail yellow flowers that would normally be crushed underfoot.

"Amazing," I said in awe.

"What?" asked Josh.

"There's a chance that no human being has ever set foot here before," I said.

"Don't say that!" Josh cried.

"Can't you appreciate it?" I asked.

"Why do I get the feeling this is something we're not going to appreciate for long?" Andy moaned.

"Just tell us which way to go," Josh pleaded.

I looked around. We could go in a dozen different directions. But only one would lead us back to the camp.

"See?" Josh said bitterly. "The great Jake doesn't know which way to go, either."

I pointed into the woods. "That way. South."

"Why south?" Andy asked.

"If we go that way, the sun will be on our right," I explained. "On the flight up here the sun was mostly on our left. The other thing is, it looks like it might be slightly downhill, which could lead us to water."

"That sounds good," said Andy.

"Oh, yeah? Then how come Ted went in *that* direction?" Josh pointed in the opposite direction, north.

Andy bit his lip and gave me a worried look. "How come, Jake?"

"I think Ted went in that direction because . . ." I knew I had to come up with a reason fast, or Andy was going to freak. "Because he was trying to trick us. He figured we might try to follow him back to camp, so he decided to lead us in the wrong direction and get us really lost."

Josh made a disbelieving face. "Bull."

Andy looked like he didn't know who to believe.

"I have to go with my gut feeling," I said. "And that's south."

"I'm going with my *brain*," countered Josh. "And my brain says I'd be totally insane to follow you instead of Ted."

Andy looked back and forth between us. "Come on, guys. You have to agree."

"I think Josh is wrong," I said.

"Well, I think *you're* wrong," Josh shot back stubbornly.

"Oh, great!" Andy cried. "Here I am, a million miles from anywhere with my two nut-brain friends who can't agree which way to go! Why wait to die? Why don't I just dig a hole and bury myself right now? I know why! Because I don't have a shovel. I have to make one! How's that for ironic?"

"Come with me, Andy," Josh urged him.

Andy looked at me. "If I go with Josh, will you come, too?"

I shook my head.

"He's full of it," Josh scoffed. "The second you and I leave, he'll come running after us like a little lost puppy."

"Try me," I said.

Josh wrinkled his forehead and gave me a hard look. "Okay, Jake, if that's the way you want it." He turned to Andy. "Let's go."

Andy still wouldn't budge.

"Listen, guys, we can spend all day arguing," I said. "I'd really like you to come with me, but either way, I'm out of here."

I turned and headed into the woods. In the shade of the trees, the air felt cooler and damper. A second later I heard the crash of footsteps behind me.

It was Andy. "I sure hope you know what you're doing, Jake."

"So do I," I replied.

25

There was no trail to follow. Just brown tree trunks, green underbrush, rotting logs, and gray lichen-covered rocks.

"Hey, wait!" a familiar voice cried behind us as Josh came crashing through the brush. "I can't believe you'd just leave me!"

"We didn't leave you," I said. "You didn't want to come."

Josh chose to ignore that. "This is the wrong way, Jake. I know it is. I can feel it in my gut."

"Then why'd you come?" Andy asked.

"Because I'm a total chicken," Josh admitted. "I'd rather die wrong with my friends than live right and alone."

"We're not going to die," I said.

"Want to bet ten bucks?" Josh asked.

Andy tapped him on the shoulder. "Has it occurred to you that if you win this bet you won't be able to collect?"

"Shut up," Josh grumbled.

It was slow going through the forest. We had to pick our way through the trees, over the fallen logs, and around patches of brier and other thorny undergrowth. Even though it was shady in the woods, we were soon sweating.

"I wouldn't mind something to eat and drink," Andy said.

"How can you think about food at a time like this?" Josh asked in disbelief.

"I'm hungry and thirsty," Andy complained. Suddenly he stopped. "Wait! You guys hear something?"

"Yes," said Josh. "I hear a little voice in my head saying, 'Next time you go to camp, Josh, make sure *you* pick the camp and not that bonehead Jake.'"

"I'm serious," Andy said.

"So am I," replied Josh.

"Hey," I said. "I hear it, too. It sounds like running water."

We followed the sound and came to a stream. After taking long drinks of the fresh, cold water, I suggested that we camp there for the night.

"Why don't we just keep going?" Josh asked. "The faster we get out of here, the better."

"No, Jake's right," said Andy. "It'll be dark in a few hours. If we stop now and make camp, we'll get a good night's rest and be ready to go in the morning."

Andy started to pull off his hiking boots.

"What are you doing?" Josh asked.

"I'm gonna wade into the stream and look for crayfish under the rocks," he said.

"Then I better try to start a fire so we can cook them," I said.

Josh put his hands on his hips. "I guess that means I have to build a shelter."

It took me a long time to make a bow drill and fire board from a stick, a shoelace, and a small chunk of wood, but I finally managed to do it. Then, after about a hundred tries, I actually lit some thin strips of beech bark. By adding bigger and bigger sticks, I got a real fire going.

And just in time, too. The sun was starting to go down.

I was putting rocks around the fire to keep it contained when Andy jogged back from the stream. His day pack was filled with squirmy, kicking crayfish. "Hey, Jake! Check this out! I got dinner!"

By then Josh had finished making a shelter out of pine branches. As it grew dark, we settled around the fire and roasted the crayfish on small pointed sticks.

"What I wouldn't give for some melted butter to dunk these crayfish in," Andy said as he ate.

"What I wouldn't give for a cheeseburger," Josh added with despair.

"Shouldn't we just be glad we've got something to eat?" I asked.

"You're right," Andy agreed apologetically.

"Just promise me," Josh said. "No Uncle Remus stories about Brer Rabbit tonight."

"And let's all pray that a big grizzly doesn't come," added Andy.

No sooner were the words out of his mouth than we heard rustling sounds from the woods.

Andy straightened up. "What was that?"

"Probably just an animal," I said.

The rustling sounds grew louder.

"A *big* animal," Josh said nervously as his eyes darted to the left and right.

"The fire should keep it away," I said, trying to stay calm but feeling pretty nervous myself.

Crack! A branch snapped in the dark. It couldn't have been more than a dozen feet away.

Andy jumped to his feet. "I don't know what kind of animal that is!" he gasped. "But the fire sure doesn't bother it!"

26

Josh and I got to our feet. The rustling sounds were coming closer. What could we do? We had no weapons, no experience fighting wild animals . . .

"Ahhhhhhh!" Andy screamed.

Out of the shadows came . . . me.

"Jake?" Josh gasped.

"Ted," replied Ted in my body.

He glanced around at the shelter, the fire, and the pile of crayfish shells left from our dinner.

"You did this all by yourselves?" he seemed surprised.

"Hey, he's right!" Andy gasped as if suddenly realizing what we'd done. "We've been surviving!"

Josh puffed out his chest proudly. "Yeah, and *you* didn't think we could do anything."

"Right," I said angrily to Ted in my body. "You left us to die."

"So why'd you come back anyway?" Josh asked.

Ted in my body shrugged. "I . . . I couldn't leave you helpless."

"Let me ask you something," Josh said. "When you left us in the clearing, why'd you head north?"

"I . . . I . . ." Ted in my body didn't seem to know what to say.

"You were trying to trick us," I said. "So if we followed you we'd get even more lost."

Ted nodded my head slowly. "I'm sorry. I was angry. I wanted to teach you a lesson."

"Wait a minute! I know why you came back!" Josh cried accusingly. "You realized that if Jake in your body croaked in the woods, you'd never get your body back. For the rest of your life you'd be stuck in Jake's miserable excuse for a body."

"Hey!" I yelled angrily. "That's *my* body you're talking about."

"Is that why you wouldn't give Ted his body back?" Andy asked me.

I nodded.

"No! I, uh, never thought of that," protested Ted in my body.

My friends and I gave him a get-real look.

Ted in my body sighed. "Oh, okay, you're right. I wouldn't want to be stuck in this body. So now that I'm here, can I *please* have my body back?"

I shook my head. "How do we know you won't leave us again?"

"I promise," said Ted.

"That's not good enough," said Josh.

"What else can I do?" asked Ted in my body.

"What can he do for us?" I asked.

"What's the one thing we want more than anything else?" Andy asked.

"I know!" Josh suddenly smiled. "Pizza!"

27

"**Y**ou mean, you want to try to *win* the Ultimate Challenge?" Andy asked.

"Why not?" Josh answered. "We just proved we could survive, didn't we?"

"But what do you want pizza for?" asked Ted in my body.

"We want pizza," Josh began, "because we're not mutants like *you*. We don't get a charge out of eating tree bark and roots and weeds. We want pizza because we're normal. That's why."

Ted shook my head. "I'll be honest. I'd like to help you win, but I don't see how we can. We're too far behind. The other teams have a head start on us."

"Sounds like a negative attitude to me," I said with a wink.

"Yeah," agreed Andy. "If you think we're gonna go through all this and *still* eat fish and berries when we get back, you're mental."

"But the only way to win would be to slow the other teams down," argued Ted in my body. "We can't. We don't know where they are. It would be like trying to find a needle in a haystack."

My friends and I shared a frustrated look.

"Wait a minute!" Josh cried. "There *is* a way we *can* find them!"

"How?" asked Andy.

Josh turned to Ted and held out his hand. "Give me the CPP."

"No!" protested Ted in my body. "You can't have it. You're not allowed. It's for emergencies only."

"This *is* an emergency," Josh insisted. "It's what I call a *food* emergency. This is an If-I-don't-get-that-pizza-someone's-gonna-die kind of emergency. And that someone might just be me."

Ted in my body gave me in his body a questioning look.

"Hand it over," I said.

He took out the CPP and tossed it to Josh, who flicked it on. Andy and I looked over his shoulder. On the screen we could see three glowing yellow dots and one glowing red dot.

"Each of the yellow dots represents one team," Ted explained. "We're the red dot. The closest yellow dot is approximately half a mile southwest of us. It's not moving so that means they've probably settled down for the night."

"What are we going to do?" Andy asked.

"We're going to go on a little night mission," Josh replied with a smile. He headed into the woods.

Ted in my body turned to me in his. "Now that I've agreed to help you guys, can I get my body back?"

"Not until I smell pizza," I answered, and followed Josh.

28

"**T**his is completely against the rules," protested Ted in my body as we snuck through the woods in the dark. Josh was in the lead, keeping one eye on the CPP.

"If you don't shut up, I'm going to make sure Jake *never* gives your body back," Josh threatened.

"Or, at least, not until I've stuffed it with pizza," I said.

"Full of fat hormones and growth chloresterals," Josh added.

"Of course, if I stuff *your* body with pizza then I'll still be hungry when I get back into mine," I mused.

Josh stopped and sniffed. "What's that smell?"

Slight wisps of a strange odor wafted toward us in the night air. I couldn't quite figure out what it was.

"Smoke?" I guessed.

"Smoke and something else," suggested Ted in my body.

"P-U," I said. "It stinks."

"Whatever it is, it means we must be getting close," Andy whispered.

Sure enough, through the woods ahead, we caught a glimpse of some faintly glowing coals, as if a small fire was burning itself out.

"Hey, Mr. Night Vision," Josh whispered. "Can you tell which team it is?"

Ted in my body squinted into the dark. "Uh, I can't see."

"That's because you're not Mr. Night Vision anymore," Josh smirked. "Jake in your body is."

I peered through the dark. "Judging from the running shoes outside their shelter it must be the Forest Runners."

"Good," said Josh. "Then it's time to begin Operation Lace Erase. Come with me, Jake."

Josh led me in Ted's body through the woods toward the campsite. Morgan's team was nestled in a shelter made of pine branches. Their running shoes were lined up outside.

The closer we got, the stronger the odor got. It was one of the most acrid, yucky smells I'd ever encountered.

"What *is* that stink?" I whispered.

"Maybe they burned some green wood or something," Josh guessed.

By now we were holding our noses and wiping tears from our burning eyes.

"Josh," I whispered. "I don't think I can take it anymore!"

"We *have* to!" Josh insisted. "Think of that pizza."

Imagining a pizza with a crispy crust, gooey cheese, and sausage and meatball toppings did the trick. Despite the horrible odor, I followed Josh to the row of running shoes.

"Get the laces," Josh whispered.

As I bent over the first pair of running shoes, the stink was so powerful I could hardly breathe. Suddenly I realized what it was.

Foot odor!

"Those girls probably haven't washed their feet or changed their socks in three weeks!" I wheezed.

"I know!" Josh gasped. "It's a real killer! Grab the laces and let's get out of here!"

A few minutes later, we rejoined Andy and Ted in the woods. Back at our own campsite, we sacked out for the night.

The next morning we were up with the sun.

"I'm starved," Josh yawned as he stretched.

"Me, too," Andy said.

"I'd skip breakfast if I were you," advised Ted in my body.

"Why?" I asked, since in Ted's body I was pretty hungry, too.

"Because if we take time to look for food, we'll never catch up with the other teams," explained Ted in my body.

"He's right," Josh said. "Okay, men, time to move out!"

Andy saluted. "In what direction, *sir*?"

Josh checked the CPP. "South!"

It wasn't long before we came to the spot where the Forest Runners had spent the night. But something was wrong.

"They're gone!" Josh gasped.

"I don't get it." Andy scratched his head. "How could they go anywhere without their running shoes?"

"They wore their shoes," replied Ted in my body.

"What did they use for shoelaces?" I asked.

"Vines." Ted in my body held up a thin, green stem.

"That's ridiculous!" Josh sputtered. "The vines will break."

"Maybe," said Ted in my body. "But if they do, they can just replace them with new vines."

Andy smirked at Josh. "Operation Lace Erase. Great idea, space brain."

"It was better than anything *you* thought up, vacuum skull," Josh shot back.

"Stop fighting, guys," I said. "We better get moving."

We started south again. For a while we followed

the Forest Runners' trail. But around noon, Josh stopped.

"What is it?" I asked.

"I know this is going to sound weird," he said, "but I think the Forest Runners went in another direction."

We all looked at Ted in my body. He nodded. "Very good, Josh. I noticed the same thing a few minutes ago. It appears the Forest Runners veered off."

"Why?" Andy asked.

"My guess is they needed to find water," Ted answered. "That's the problem with Morgan's high-carbohydrate program. It gives you a lot of energy, but it absorbs a lot of water, too."

"Weird," Josh said.

"Not really," replied Ted in my body. "Don't you get thirsty when you eat a lot of bread?"

"That's not what I meant," said Josh. "What's weird is that I don't know *how* I knew that the Forest Runners had turned. I just sort of, er, *sensed* it."

Ted in my body smiled. "You've become at one with nature."

Josh rolled his eyes. "Maybe, but what I'd really like to become at one with is that hot, crusty pizza."

We continued through the woods. Except for our footsteps, there was silence. Here and there, a shaft of sunlight poked through the thick canopy of green above us. I might have enjoyed the scenery if it weren't for the nagging hunger in my stomach and the grungy sensation of needing a shower really bad.

Suddenly the silence was broken by a shout: "Get down on your hands and knees!"

29

The shout had come out of the woods. Was it an attack? Was someone coming?

We stared into the woods in all directions.

"I don't see anyone," Josh said in a low voice.

"Over here!" Ted in my body waved us toward a big, fallen log. As we went toward him we could hear more voices. *Girls'* voices.

"I can't find them!" someone cried.

"Get down on your hands and knees . . . and look!" shouted the voice we'd heard before.

"But it's all yucky and muddy!" cried someone else.

"I don't care!"

On the other side of the big log, the Forest Runners wallowed in a muddy, swampy area. Their arms and legs were covered with dark mud. Morgan was in the middle of them.

"You have to find them!" she shouted at her team.

"Find what?" Andy whispered to us.

"Their running shoes," answered Ted in my body. "The mud must have sucked them right off their feet."

"Then Operation Lace Erase worked!" Josh gasped.

"They'll probably find their shoes sooner or later," Ted predicted. "But this will definitely slow them down."

"All right!" Josh cheered. "That's one team down, two to go. Let's go, gentlemen. Show no mercy! There's a hot, crusty pizza in our futures!"

We started through the woods again. On the CPP we could see the other three glowing yellow dots. One represented the Techno-Wizards, one the Forest Runners, and the other the Vultures.

"Which is which?" I asked as I looked over Josh's shoulder at the CPP.

"There's no way to tell," Ted informed us.

Suddenly one of the yellow dots vanished from the screen.

"What the . . . ?" Josh shook the CPP, but the yellow dot didn't reappear.

"What happened?" I asked.

"One of the other CPPs must have malfunctioned," Ted in my body guessed.

Josh pointed at the two yellow dots left on the screen.

"Then this is the team we'll try to slow down next," he said. "All right, Weed Eaters, let's keep moving!"

Our progress through the woods was slowed by thick underbrush and dense patches of thorny brier. Finally, in the late afternoon, Andy stopped to study some broken twigs.

"I think we're on their trail!" He got down on his hands and knees and searched the ground. "Yup! Here's a footprint! It's the Techno-Wizards!"

"How can you tell?" Josh asked.

Andy pointed at the footprint. "It's a hiking boot, not a motorcycle boot."

"Very good, Andy." Ted in my body congratulated him.

Andy blinked with surprise. "Gee, I guess I really *have* learned some stuff!"

We huddled in the woods. Josh flicked on the CPP. Once again, only two yellow dots glowed on the screen. "This dot must be them."

"I still wonder what happened to the Vultures," said Andy.

"Let's take care of the Techno-Wizards first," said Josh. "We'll worry about the Vultures later."

Just like the previous night, we made camp. Josh and Andy built a shelter, and I started a fire, while Ted looked for dinner.

"I'm starved," Andy groaned as he and Josh collected branches for the shelter. "We haven't eaten all day. I sure hope Ted finds something good."

"What do you think he's going to do?" Josh

asked sarcastically. "Bring back Big Macs and fries?"

"Maybe some more crayfish," Andy said hopefully.

I shook my head. "I hate to say this, guys, but we're a long way from any river. Looks like McBerries and McInsects tonight."

"I can't take it!" Josh cried. "This is gonna kill me! I'd eat just about anything! As long as it was cooked! Lamb brain tacos! Marinated dog! White ant pie! *Anything!*"

"Focus on the pizza we'll win for being the first team to get back to camp," Andy advised him. "Think about becoming at one with that pizza."

But thinking about becoming at one with a pizza wasn't the same as actually *eating* a pizza. Maybe the tinder I was using was damp. Or maybe I was distracted by hunger. Either way, I had a really hard time starting a fire.

"I don't know what to do, guys," I said. "I can't get a fire started."

"Why don't you check Ted's backpack?" Josh suggested. "I bet he has matches."

"No way," said Andy. "Cal would never let anyone use matches."

"I bet he secretly gave them to the counselors," Josh said. "In case of emergency. Just like the CPPs."

"You think?" I asked uncertainly.

"Can't hurt to look," said Josh.

I unzipped Ted's pack and stuck my hand in. I was feeling around for matches when my hand hit something long and thin and covered by a plastic wrapper. I pulled it out.

"I don't believe it!" I gasped.

Andy turned and saw what was in my hands. "Beef jerky!" he cried.

Josh spun around. "Where?"

Andy pointed at me.

Half-crazed with hunger, my friends instantly pounced! A split second later, we were in a three-way wrestling match.

"I gotta have it!" Josh cried desperately.

"It's mine!" I yelled. "I found it!"

We rolled around on the forest floor, fighting over the beef jerky. Suddenly Josh pushed Andy away, and he and I got into a beef jerky tug-of-war.

Snap! The plastic wrapper tore in half. Josh and I fell backward. Even before I hit the ground I was stuffing my half of the jerky into my mouth.

"No fair!" Andy cried. "I didn't get any!"

Josh and I didn't answer. We were too busy panting for breath and chewing as fast as we could.

Andy dashed back to Ted's pack. He held it upside down and dumped everything on the ground. Josh and I went slack-jawed as more beef jerkies fell out!

"Aha!" Andy cried gleefully.

Crash! We all dove on the pile.

Once again we were wrestling. "Gimme that!" "It's mine!" "I *need* it!"

It wasn't long before each of us had three or four jerkies. We huddled in opposite corners of the campsite, our cheeks bulging as we frantically devoured the food. I was so busy shoving beef jerky into my mouth that I accidentally ate part of Ted's beard and mustache, too!

"I can't believe Ted had this stuff," Andy sputtered through a half-chewed mouthful.

"Yeah," I agreed. "These things are made from meat. They're filled with nitrates and preservatives. Ted swore he'd never touch stuff like this."

"Well, I've got news for you," Josh said with bulging cheeks. "Ted's a total bald-faced phony."

"No wonder he never complained about the berries and roots," Andy grumbled angrily. "He was probably sneaking these things all along!"

"That environmental hypocrite!" Josh added.

We heard a stick crack somewhere close by.

"Chill, guys," I whispered. "Here he comes!"

My friends and I quickly scooped up the jerky wrappers and stuffed them in our pockets. A moment later, Ted in my body came out of the woods.

"Bad news, guys." He looked grim. "All I could find was some roots and tree bark. It won't make much of a meal."

My friends and I nodded in mock sympathy.

"Sometimes you just have to go hungry," I said.

"The important thing is to stick to your beliefs," added Josh.

"You can't forget about the big environmental picture," added Andy.

Ted in my body nodded. "I'm glad you guys understand. In the long run it'll make the world a better place. And you'll be better human beings."

"Like you, Ted?" Andy asked innocently.

"I try," Ted replied earnestly. "That's all anyone can do."

"Oh, yeah?" Josh held up an empty beef jerky wrapper. "Maybe there is something else you can do. You can talk like a righteous environmentalist Save-the-Earth vegetarian and then sneak off at night and eat beef jerky while the rest of your team starves."

Ted in my body turned pale. "You . . . you didn't happen to leave *just one* for me, did you?"

My friends and I grinned and shook our heads.

30

I can't say we enjoyed watching Ted in my body eat roots and tree bark for dinner. In fact, it was kind of pitiful. He admitted that while he sincerely *believed* it was wrong to eat meats and processed foods, he found it impossible to live that way.

"I mean," he said, "in a perfect world, we'd all be better off if we ate less red meat and more vegetables."

"Right," agreed Josh. "And in a perfect world we never would have come to this crazy camp in the first place."

"Know what, Ted?" Andy said.

Ted stiffened, as if he expected Andy to criticize him.

"Now that I know you're not perfect," Andy said, "I like you better."

Josh and I nodded in agreement.

"In fact," Andy continued, "I feel bad that we ate all your beef jerky and didn't leave you some."

Ted in my body actually looked like he was blinking back tears. He turned to Josh and me. "You mean it, guys?"

Josh and I glanced at each other. I'm not sure either of us would have gone *that* far. But we gave him halfhearted nods anyway.

Ted bit into a piece of bark and started to chew. "Know what, guys? I've had campers with better wilderness skills than you, but I've never had campers with more heart. How about a group hug?"

My friends and I traded wary looks.

"Maybe another time," Josh said.

"Yeah," agreed Andy. "Let's not go overboard."

Shortly after sunset we mobilized Operation Compass Swipe.

"Without their compasses those guys will be helpless," Josh whispered as we snuck through the dark woods and hid behind the trees just outside the Techno-Wizards' camp. It wasn't long before the Wizards finished dinner and crawled into their shelter. Moments later we could hear them snoring.

"They must be really tired," Andy whispered.

Josh turned to Ted in my body. "Okay, Mr. I-Never-Touch-Red-Meat. Go in there and take their compasses."

Ted in my body crept off silently. It was spooky how noiselessly he could sneak through the woods and into their shelter.

A moment later, he returned with the compasses. We started back through the dark to our camp.

"That's two teams down and one to go," Andy said. "All we have to do now is slow down the Vultures and that pizza dinner is ours."

Suddenly Ted in my body froze. We quickly saw why. Someone was sitting at our campfire, roasting a marshmallow on a stick.

It was Axel!

He looked up at us and bared his teeth. The light from the fire's flames reflected off his gold tooth. "Did I hear someone say something about slowing down the Vultures?"

We heard sounds behind us. The rest of the Vultures came out of the dark forest. They were carrying wooden clubs.

31

Tapping the clubs against their palms, the Vultures stepped toward us. My friends and I formed a tight circle with our backs pressed together.

Meanwhile, Axel slowly pushed himself up. "Know what's funny?"

"Uh, a two-hundred-pound parakeet named Hank?" Andy guessed.

"No, dummy," Axel grumbled. "I meant about you guys sabotaging the Forest Runners and the Techno-Wizards."

"What?" asked Ted in my body.

"I thought the Vultures were going to have to do all that work," said Axel. "But you guys made our job easy. You did it for us."

"Well, uh, then I think it's only fair that we all share the pizza dinner," I said.

Axel frowned at me. "Since when do *you* eat pizza, Teddy Bear? I thought you only ate moldy bean sprouts and caterpillars."

"Er, I was thinking about my team," I quickly replied.

Axel grinned. "Well, ain't that cute. The trouble is, I'm thinking about *my* team. And I happen to know that none of them wants to share their pizzas with a bunch of weed-eating wimps."

"That's alliteration!" Andy said brightly.

"Shut up!" Axel yelled at him.

"So what are you going to do to us?" Josh asked.

Axel scratched his head. "Good question."

"We could tie 'em all to a tree and leave 'em for the wolves," suggested Toothpick.

My friends and I exchanged frightened looks.

"At least it's not the brier patch," mumbled Ted in my body.

"What'd he say?" asked Axel.

"Something about a brier patch," another Vulture answered with a shrug.

"Maybe we could shove 'em in a bear cave and block it up behind them," suggested the fourth Vulture.

"Even *that* would be better than the brier patch," sighed Ted in my body.

Axel turned toward him. "What's with you and this brier patch?"

"Nothing!" Ted in my body gasped fearfully.

"How about we tie 'em up and set 'em adrift on

a raft on a lake?" suggested Toothpick. "Then the alligators'll get 'em."

"There are no alligators around here, stupid," Axel snarled. "Besides, I know what we're gonna do. Follow me."

32

Using a flashlight, Axel and his Vultures led us through the dark woods.

"I thought flashlights weren't allowed," I said.

"Don't talk," Axel said.

"Where are you taking us?" Josh asked nervously.

"Be quiet," Axel ordered.

"You guys aren't playing by the rules," Andy complained.

"Shut up!" Axel shouted.

Andy gave me a terrified look. All the horribilities of what we were about to face flitted through my mind — a snake pit, quicksand, a bear den. My heart started to beat hard and my mouth went dry. This was probably it. The end of my life. Just as I'd feared, we were all going to perish in the wilderness. And all because I'd gotten the stupid name of the camp mixed up!

Ahead of us, Axel stopped and swept the flashlight beam over a thick patch of overgrown green vegetation.

"What is it?" asked Toothpick.

"It's a brier patch, dummy," Axel answered. "See all those thorns and stickers?" With a nasty grin he turned to Ted in my body. "I bet this is the *last* thing you wanted to see, right, Jake?"

Suddenly I realized why Ted in my body had been dropping hints about the brier patch. That was exactly how Brer Rabbit tricked Brer Fox!

Meanwhile, Ted in my body pretended to tremble. "Don't!" he begged hoarsely. "Not the brier patch! Please, anything but *that*!"

Axel just kept grinning. "Tough luck, pal." Then he turned to his team. "Throw 'em in, guys."

33

"**O**w, OW, *OW*!" Andy cried in the dark. "This hurts!"

"Yikes!" screamed Josh. "Ouch!"

They'd thrown all of us in the brier patch. Sharp thorns and prickles were sticking into my body in a thousand different places. Meanwhile, the Vultures were laughing and patting each other on the back.

"Way to go, Axel!"

"That'll slow 'em down."

"Okay, dudes," Axel said. "Let's get back to that nice shelter the Weed Wimps were so kind to build for us. We'll get some sleep and head out in the morning. By tomorrow night we'll be chowing down on a big pizza dinner."

The Vultures disappeared into the dark woods, leaving us in our prison of briers.

"Guys, you okay?" whispered Ted in my body.

"Are you *crazy*?" cried Andy. "How could we be okay? We're getting stuck all over!"

"Why'd you want Axel to throw us in this stuff?" Josh wailed.

"It worked for Brer Rabbit," replied Ted in my body.

"Well, we're *not* rabbits, okay?" Josh cried. "We weren't born *or* bred in a brier patch. And right now we're in total pain."

"Keep your voice down," I hissed.

"Drop dead, Jake," Josh muttered. "This is all your fault. If it wasn't for you we wouldn't be in this mess."

"Will you give that up already?" I shot back. "I've told you a hundred times I'm sorry."

"It's not enough," Josh yelped. "Sorry doesn't get the thorns out of my butt."

"I hate to bring this back to reality," interrupted Andy, "but does anybody know how to get out of this stuff?"

"Just follow me," said Ted in my body.

"Follow you?" Josh cried. "I can't even *blink* without getting stuck by a million thorns. How am I supposed to follow you?"

"Just do it!" I hissed.

Moaning, groaning, and frequently yelping with pain, we followed Ted in my body out of the brier patch. Finally we reached a small clearing. The moonlight glistened on the little drops of blood seeping out of our scratches.

"I'm bleeding all over!" Andy moaned.

"We all are," replied Ted in my body. "But they're minor cuts and scratches. They won't stop us."

"Stop us from what?" I asked.

"From getting our revenge," Ted grumbled.

34

We spent most of the night bending young trees over until they were nearly looped double. Then we tied snares to their tops. It was hard work in the dark and we didn't finish until early morning. By then, the sky was turning gray with dawn. We were bleary, tired, and hungry.

"How many snares do you think we set?" Josh asked.

"At least thirty," answered Ted in my body. "Maybe more."

"I just hope I can remember where they all are," Andy said with a yawn.

"Boy, I'm so hungry I could eat a pizza all by myself," Ted in my body groaned.

My friends and I stared at him in shock. "What'd you say?"

Ted in my body blinked with astonishment. "I, uh, I didn't mean it, I swear! All I want is a nice, juicy apple!"

Andy, Josh, and I shared a wink. "*Sure*, Ted."

We hid behind the trees and waited for the Vultures to wake up. Ted in my body was hiding near me.

"Hey, Ted," I whispered. "You never told me what happened last summer that made Axel so mad."

"I told him he had the brains of a rock," Ted in my body whispered back.

"That's *all*?" I asked.

"He's very sensitive about stuff like that," Ted in my body replied.

It wasn't long before the Vultures crawled out of their shelter and started into the forest. It was obvious that they were eager to get back to camp and enjoy that pizza dinner.

As they came through the woods toward us, I stepped out from behind a tree. "Hey, Axel, you big dork!"

Axel's jaw fell when he saw me. "Ted? How'd you get out of the brier patch?"

"Slowly," Andy yelled and stepped out from behind another tree. "And with a lot of pain, thanks to you, you dumb jerk!"

Axel's eyes narrowed angrily.

"But it's okay," Josh added as he stepped out from behind a third tree, "because now we're going to beat you hairy lard-brains back to camp. You can watch us eat pizza tonight."

Axel turned to the rest of the Vultures and shouted, "Get 'em!"

The Vultures thrashed through the woods toward us. We Weed Eaters immediately spread out and headed toward the tree snares we'd set during the night. Axel was coming after me as I wove a crooked course through the snares.

Sproing! I heard a snare trip somewhere in the woods. That meant one Vulture was caught.

Sproing! Sproing! I counted two more.

Sproing! That was it! Four *sproings* meant Axel and his Vultures were all caught!

I stopped and turned around.

Just as I expected, two of the Vultures were now hanging upside down from the tops of trees, flailing their arms in a vain effort to get free.

I heard more thrashing sounds and looked in another direction, expecting to see Axel and Toothpick also hanging from trees.

But I was in for a surprise.

35

Instead of finding Axel and Toothpick hanging upside down from trees, I found Ted in my body and Andy!

"What happened?" I gasped.

"I *told* you I couldn't remember where all the snares were," Andy answered miserably.

I turned to Ted in my body. "You're supposed to be the expert at this stuff! What's *your* excuse?"

"I just couldn't stop thinking about that pizza," he moped.

If Ted in my body and Andy were hanging from trees, that meant Axel and Toothpick were still on the ground.

Meanwhile, the only free Weed Eater besides me was Josh. I looked around, but all I saw was woods.

"Josh!" I called. "Where are you?"

"Over here." Josh stepped out from behind a tree.

"Come on!" I yelled. "You have to help me get our guys down."

"Think again, Weed Wimp," a voice snarled.

I spun around. Axel and Toothpick were standing behind me, holding wooden clubs.

"You're not getting anyone down," Axel growled as he slapped the club against his palm. "Because you're about to become roadkill."

In the tree where he was hanging upside down, Andy cleared his throat. "Uh, excuse me, but he can't become roadkill if there are no roads around here."

Axel ignored him and nodded to Toothpick. "You get the one with the red hair," he said, meaning Josh. "I'll get Teddy Bear."

They started toward us. I glanced nervously at Josh. We had no weapons and no training in hand-to-hand combat.

"What are we gonna do?" I asked.

"I don't know about you, but I know what I'm going to do." Josh turned and stepped into the nearest unsprung snare.

Sproing! He shot up into the tree and hung there upside down.

"Why'd you do that?" I cried.

"Because it beats getting turned into roadkill," Josh answered.

"He's right." Axel turned his nasty grin toward me. "Now it's two against one, Teddy Bear. Your friend just made our job a whole lot easier."

36

I took off through the woods. There were more snares, and hopefully Axel and Toothpick didn't know where they were.

Sproing! I heard another snare go off behind me. Looking around, I saw Toothpick shoot into the air and hang there upside down, flailing.

"Very good, Teddy Bear!" Axel yelled behind me. "Now it's just me and you."

"Actually it's *you* and *me*," Andy called in the distance.

Luckily Ted's body was in good shape, and I managed to stay ahead of Axel in the woods.

"What's the point of running, Teddy Bear?" Axel called behind me. "It's not gonna help get your team back to camp any sooner. Your only choice is to stop and fight."

He was right. As long as the rest of the Weed Eaters were hanging from the trees, we couldn't win. On the other hand, I didn't see how I could win in a fight with Axel.

But I stopped running anyway. "Okay, Axel, I'll fight you."

"You will?" Axel looked surprised.

"I just need some time to psych myself up," I said.

Axel gave me a suspicious look. "Is this a trick?"

"No way," I said. "All I want to do is go back to the shelter and listen to a tape."

Axel frowned. "What kind of tape?"

"Uh, self-help," I replied.

"Self-help for *fighting*?" Axel scowled.

"Sure," I said. "Why not?"

Axel scratched his jaw and thought. "Well, okay. But I'm coming with you."

37

We went back to the shelter. By now, the fire from the night before had burned out. All that was left was a ring of rocks around a heap of cold, gray ashes.

I sat down and took the mini-DITS out of my day pack.

Axel smirked. "You really think listening to some tape is gonna help you in a fight?"

"It's the only chance I have," I answered.

"If that's your only chance, you're out of luck, sucker." Axel chuckled meanly.

In desperation I slipped on the mini-DITS headphones. What could I do to beat Axel? What would Ted do? What would Uncle Remus have Brer Rabbit do?

I had an idea. Adjusting a dial on the mini-DITS, I pretended to turn up the volume.

I began to chant: "Murder. Maim. Kill."

I jumped to my feet and started to pump myself up, grunting "Kill! Massacre! Destroy!"

Clenching my fists and curling my arms like the Incredible Hulk, I gritted my teeth and made my eyes bulge. "Kill! KILL! *KILL!*"

Out of the corner of my eye I watched Axel scowl at first and then begin to look worried.

"KILL! KILL! KILL!" I screamed.

Axel jumped up. "What the heck are you listening to?" He grabbed the other set of headphones and pulled them on.

This was my chance! I quickly looked around for something to switch Axel with. But there was nothing!

Just the dead ashes from the fire, and the rocks, and the shelter, and —

Wait a minute!

Some of those rocks were about the same size as a human head!

"I don't hear nothin'." Axel adjusted the headphones. "What is this?"

I yanked off my headphones and jammed them down on one of the head-sized rocks.

"What the . . . ?" Axel grunted.

I pushed the button on the mini-DITS.

Whump!

38

"What happened?" asked Ted in my body as I cut the snare that was holding him up in the tree.

"I remembered that you said Axel had the brains of a rock," I said.

"So?"

"I guess you weren't kidding." I moved on to Andy's tree and helped him down.

A few minutes later, my friends and I were back at the shelter. Axel was standing exactly where I'd left him with a stony expression on his face. He hadn't moved an inch.

Ted in my body looked down at the rock with the headphones on it. He winced. "You switched him with a *rock*?"

"Not a lot of difference as far as I can see," Andy commented with a shrug.

"He just doesn't move as much," added Josh.

"Now what?" asked Ted in my body.

Toothpick and the other Vultures were still

hanging from the trees. They were shocked when we cut them down and told them we wanted to share the victory pizza dinner with them.

All they had to do in return was help Josh and me get Axel and the rock back to camp. Then I gave Andy the Forest Runners' shoelaces and the CPP and told him to go find them and give them their shoelaces back. I did the same thing with Ted in my body and the Techno-Wizards' compasses.

"We'll all meet in the woods outside the camp just before dinnertime," I said.

Ted in my body started into the woods, then stopped. "Wait a minute," he said. "Can I have my body back now?"

"Not yet," I said.

39

Just before dinner we met the other teams in the woods outside camp. Philip, the head of the Techno-Wizards, and Morgan, the head of the Forest Runners, looked puzzled.

"I don't get it, Ted," Morgan said to me. "Why'd you help us? Now the Weed Eaters won't win."

"Yes, we will," I said.

We lined up by teams with the Weed Eaters in front and marched back into camp.

Cal was waiting for us in front of the big tent. His arms were crossed and he was nodding slowly.

"Very interesting, Ted," he said.

"How come you're not surprised?" I asked.

Cal held up a CPP. "I've been following the team movements since the beginning. I have to admit that it was pretty confusing at first. But in the end I figured it out. Your Weed Eaters managed to surprise me after all."

"We were the first back to the camp," I said.

"That means we get the pizza dinner. Only we're going to share it with the rest of the teams."

"That means you'll each get a lot less," Cal warned me.

"Yeah," I said. "That's exactly what it means."

40

"**I** can't believe you guys came in first," Martin said later as we sat around a big campfire, eating pizza.

"How come you helped the other teams, Ted?" Jeremy asked.

I was still in Ted's body. "Because, like Cal said, this isn't a game. It's survival. And surviving isn't about beating your fellowman. It's about helping everyone make it."

"I thought it was about being at one with nature," said Martin.

"Yeah, that's important," I agreed. "But what's *really* important is being at one with other human beings." I held up a hot crusty slice with sausage and meatball toppings and took a big bite. "And eating pizza on a regular basis."

41

After dinner, Ted and I switched back to our old bodies. Ted admitted that the pizza, chips, and soda were the best things he'd tasted in years.

"I guess I'll have to make an exception for them once in a while," he said.

We switched Axel and the rock, too. The funny thing was, nobody noticed the difference.

The next morning, Ted hung out with us while we packed up for the trip home.

"Guys, I have to admit," he said with a smile, "that you got a lot closer to nature than I ever expected."

"You're telling me," Josh replied. "If I don't take a shower and wash all this dirt off soon, stuff's going to start growing on me."

"Is there anything else you want to admit?" Andy asked our counselor.

"Well, I wouldn't mind if you gave me some of those secret video game codes you mentioned," Ted said.

Martin and Jeremy went up to Ted.

"Thanks for not picking me to go on the Ultimate Challenge," Martin said.

"And I'm sorry I ran away," added Jeremy.

"Really?" Ted asked.

"Well, no." Jeremy grinned. "But I figured I'd say it anyway."

Ted turned to Andy and me. "Do you feel like you learned anything?"

"I learned that when the going gets tough, the tough go shopping," said Andy.

"And if I ever grow a beard," I said, "I'll try not to eat it."

Later, Dewey drove us home in the truck. When we got back to the Jeffersonville mall, our parents were all waiting for us.

"You've lost weight!" Mrs. Hopka gasped when she saw how skinny Josh was.

"Hey, what do you expect?" Mr. Hopka chuckled. "He's been trying to live on camp food."

"You're so dirty!" Mrs. Kent sounded alarmed when she saw Andy.

"Big deal," scoffed Mr. Kent. "I never washed when I went to camp, either."

"Did you have fun?" my mother asked me.

"Of course he did!" exclaimed my father before I could answer. "Summer camp is *always* fun. I bet you boys can't wait to go back next year. Am I right?"

My friends and I traded a doubtful look.

280

"Know what's weird?" said Andy. "Now that it's over, in a strange way I'm sort of glad we did it."

"You mean, because we learned stuff we probably never would have learned at a camp with video games and food from McDonald's?" I guessed.

Andy and Josh nodded.

"Does that mean we might actually want to go back to Camp Grimley next year?" I asked.

Andy looked at Josh. Josh looked at me. I looked at Andy. All at once we shouted, "No way!"

ABOUT THE AUTHOR

Todd Strasser has written many award-winning
novels for young and teenage readers. Among his
best-known books are *Help! I'm Trapped in Obedience School* and *Abe Lincoln for Class President.* His most recent books for Scholastic are
Help! I'm Trapped in Obedience School Again
and *Help! I'm Trapped in an Alien's Body.*

Todd speaks frequently at schools about the
craft of writing and conducts writing workshops
for young people. He and his family live outside
New York City with their yellow Labrador
retriever, Mac.

You can find out more about Todd and his books
at http://www.toddstrasser.com